The Night Watch

Sarah Healey

PHOENIX PRESS LTD

Published 2018
PHOENIX PRESS LTD
A New Haven Publishing imprint
www.newhavenpublishingltd.com
newhavenpublishing@gmail.com

All Rights Reserved
The rights of Sarah Healey, as the author of this work, have been asserted in accordance with the Copyrights, Designs and Patents Act 1988.
No part of this book may be re-printed or reproduced or utilized in any form or by any electronic, mechanical or other means, now unknown or hereafter invented, including photocopying, and recording, or in any information storage or retrieval system, without the written permission of the Author and Publisher.
All characters and events in this publication, other than those clearly in the public domain, are fictitious and any resemblance to any company or real persons, living or dead, is purely coincidental.

Cover design © Pete Cunliffe
pcunliffe@blueyonder.co.uk

Copyright © 2018 Sarah Healey
All rights reserved
ISBN: 978-1-912587-11-7

Cast of Characters

The Police

Nick Toft, a custody sergeant
Rose Olding, a detective
Hal Petersen, a detective
Sophie Frank, a detective
Jesse Butland, a detective
Tomas Ehlen, a detective
Connor Whealdon, a constable
Lasky, a constable
Kyle and Ash, constables
Katrina and Aaron, custodians

The Prisoners

Georgia Lane, a lady
Annette McAllister, a lady
Jack McAllister, a gentleman
Brian Dunn, a drunkard
Alan Stamper, a drunkard
Alice and Jerome, two thieves
Four ne'er-do-well boys

Act One

The Suspects

1

"It's Bedlam here tonight," said David. "You'll wish you'd rung in sick."

It certainly looked like being a lively shift. Buzzed in from the car park, Nick edged down the corridor past the holding benches, where a skinny youth in handcuffs sat smirking beside a nervous young PC who looked like he might throw up. From the cells beyond came a confused cacophony of female voices, shouting to one another, swearing and occasionally wailing. Nick stepped into the main custody area to find a pool of vomit on the floor and a cleaner slowly advancing on it with a grey string mop. David was behind the tall desk, handing back property and scowling.

Nick was ten minutes early for his shift, but as he slipped behind the desk David said: "I'm finishing this one and then I'm off. It's been a long fucking day." He was returning property to a tousled young man who was being released, and there was a lot of property to return: David was ripping open clear plastic bags and tipping onto the counter piles of loose change, ticket stubs, cigarette papers, ear buds… the young man pounced on his phone when it emerged and began interrogating it with his fingers. "That's the fucking lot," David said. "Sign here."

David was one of the oldest custody sergeants and he was the most bad tempered, always either barking or muttering, his speech so barbed with expletives and sarcasm that a conversation with him was like being dragged through brambles. Nick, ever easygoing, got on with him tolerably well. "Fucking Bedlam," he was repeating now, as Nick stowed his bag and looked up at the whiteboard. The ten till six shift - the graveyard shift - was usually quiet on a Sunday night in a small town police station like this one; but the warm weather seemed to have brought out the crazies. Nick could hear a woman howling in one of the cells now - loud, rising despair echoing off hard walls. "What's going on back there?" he asked.

David shook his head.

"Lady fucking Macbeth," he said.

Nick was looking at the whiteboard on the wall beside the desk. There had been attempts by the senior staff to remove the board and insist on digital technology only, but the custody sergeants were a reactionary bunch and they liked to have everything they needed to know in plain sight, scribbled up on a board by squeaky marker pens; coming on duty, Nick could see at once the names beside the cell numbers, the arrest times, the review times, the names of the officers in charge of each case and all the little symbols and codes the custody staff used to keep the place rolling. "Right then," David was saying to the tousled young man, who had now shoved all his property into various bulging pockets. "You can fuck off now. Go to the back door and I'll buzz you out."

There were only two female names on the whiteboard: Georgia Lane and Annette McAllister. It was hard to believe that just two women were making so much noise. Nick could see from the cell numbers that they had been placed at opposite ends of the corridor; if that was a deliberate ploy to keep them from communicating, it had failed. Next to each name was written, in large letters, the acronym 'GBH' - grievous bodily harm. There was a third name on the board with the same label, a man's name.

"GBH?" asked Nick.

"Oh yeah, a serious one," nodded David. He was watching the CCTV monitor which showed the door at the end of the corridor, his hand held poised over the door release button beneath the desk top. "Likely to turn into a murder. The bloke's at the hospital now with a kitchen knife stuck in his neck."

There was an insistent buzzing sound as he pressed the door release button, and then he physically relaxed, his shoulders dropping as he mentally ended his shift. "Thank you!" he shouted sarcastically to the cleaner, who was wheeling her bucket and mop out of the room. "Took her about a fucking hour to get down here," he explained to Nick. "We're the lowest fucking priority, we are."

Nick was still studying the whiteboard. "Who's the officer in the case?" he asked. Usually the name of the officer responsible for each prisoner would appear on the board, but serious offences were investigated by CID and they worked in teams. Instead of a name, 'CID' had been scrawled up on the board.

"Oh, it's that Olding bitch. Detective Inspector Olding, she's on this one, not that she's shown her fucking face down here yet. CID, self-important twats." David was packing up his rucksack. "You know what they're like, swanning around upstairs while we clean up the vomit." He turned to the computer to sign himself out. "They've brought in a right fucking circus today."

The woman's howling had receded to an occasional yelping, but she now started up again with renewed strength.

"Is she drunk?" Nick asked.

"They've all been drinking," David said. He spoke slowly now, concentrating on the computer screen as if it was an enemy he was facing down. "All three of them. They were having a barbecue or something. A party that ended in a stabbing. She's been carrying on like that since she came in." He defeated the computer with a final click and turned away from it triumphantly. "Lady Macbeth. Seriously, they all came in here covered in blood, it was like fucking Shakespeare."

" 'Out, damned spot'?" Nick grinned.

"That's it!"

" 'Will all great Neptune's ocean wash this blood clean from my hand?' "

"What?"

Nick laughed. "My son's got his English Lit GCSE next week; I've just spent the afternoon going over *Macbeth* quotes with him."

David let out a short laugh. "Yeah, and I bet you remember it better than he does."

"Probably."

The back door buzzed again, this time a short burst to signal that somebody wanted to be let in. David glanced at the monitor and reached for the door release button. "That's Katrina," he said. "She's going to have fun tonight."

Katrina was a female custodian. On each shift the custody sergeant had custody staff to help him look after the prisoners; if there were female prisoners there had to be a female custodian. Katrina came into the room looking tired and tucking her hair mechanically behind her ears. She was a short, stocky woman with a greasy bob and a round face without makeup. She was dressed in a black t-shirt, black trousers and trainers. "Evening," she said.

"You're going to have fun tonight," David told her. He was ready to go now, his rucksack over one shoulder. He turned finally to Nick and indicated the whiteboard. "So… we've got the three for CID, the fucking bloodbath… then there's a drunk driver in six, he'll be ready to charge and release, and in seven I've put Luke Hall, he's in for breaching his bail conditions again. He's basically bedded down for the night for court tomorrow - he won't give you any trouble. And then there's someone waiting out in the corridor; don't know what that's about, don't care." He lowered his voice. "That kid of a PC looks too fucking scared to speak; you could probably leave him sat in the fucking corridor all night." He laughed. "Anyway, I'm out of here, you're welcome to it. Cheers!"

Nick buzzed David out of the building and then set about making the workspace his own. The custody suite was a bleak, hostile place of work: partially underground, like a bunker, it was a place where all the furniture was screwed down and all the surfaces could be hosed. The smell of vomit was now blended with the smell of strong disinfectant. Behind the tall desk was the sergeants' retreat, the various shelves and cubbyholes stuffed with random personal effects, although the spare jumpers and discoloured tupperware mingled with odd bits of lost property and strange paraphernalia, undocumented and unexplained: crumpled memos, an old dictaphone, a broken pager, a pair of trainers in a carrier bag. The top of the desk had to be kept clear and safe, like a demilitarised zone between hostile nations: nothing that could be used as a weapon could be left out in plain sight. There was a computer, with a sticky keyboard, a collection of pens that never worked and an aged printer that whirred morosely, the printed sheets sliding out at a snail's pace and fluttering gently into the tray, smelling of fresh ink and still slightly damp. At the back of the room was a tiny windowless kitchen, an awkward space containing a kettle and a microwave, coarse paper towels and mismatched mugs.

"I'll make us a cup of tea," mumbled Katrina.

"That'd be lovely, thanks," said Nick. He tried to catch her eye and smile at her as she slipped past him, but she was staring at the floor.

Having studied the whiteboard, Nick now turned his attention to the computer. He couldn't trust David to have told him everything: David was sloppy - a corner cutter, disdainful of rules. Nick Toft believed in doing things properly. A round shouldered, sturdy man, slightly overweight, slightly over forty, he was steady and professional; he read everything carefully, noted everything down, and explained everything clearly. He was serious, thorough, and kind. As he clicked through the details of each of the individuals now in his custody, he raised his voice to call out into the corridor: "Are you waiting to book in?"

The young constable jolted to the doorway, appearing anxiously and tumbling over his own words. "Yes sir! I've got a suspect here -"

"Okay, I'll be with you in five minutes, okay? I just need to complete the shift changeover."

The young constable nodded, swallowed, and went back to sit in the corridor.

Nick had found the arrest report for the three GBH suspects. He settled his forearms, folded on the top of the desk, and studied the small black text on the screen.

Serious Incident Report
Reporting Officer: PC 692 Chad Lohan
Date: Sunday 27 May

Attended address at 6 RIVERSIDE VIEW at 15:38 hours, in response to a report of a violent altercation inside a house. On arrival with PC 401 SYMONS we discovered the INJURED PERSON subsequently identified as CARL BRADLEY LANE DOB 07/06/88 ADDRESS 6 RIVERSIDE VIEW in the kitchen of the house. He was lying on the floor with what appeared to be the black handle of a knife protruding from the left side of his neck. He appeared to be conscious but in some distress and he was bleeding heavily. PC 401 SYMONS administered first aid and I ascertained the identities of the other individuals at the premises.

Present were:
GEORGIA LANE DOB 13/02/89 of 6 RIVERSIDE VIEW

ANNETTE MCALLISTER DOB 04/01/90 of 9 RIVERSIDE VIEW
JACK MCALLISTER DOB 20/05/85 of 9 RIVERSIDE VIEW

All three of the persons present appeared to be known to the INJURED PERSON. I observed that all three had blood on their clothing and hands. They all claimed that they had been assisting the INJURED PERSON. I formed the opinion that all three had been drinking alcohol because their eyes were glazed, their speech was slurred and I could smell alcohol on their breath. I ascertained that an ambulance had already been called and indeed it arrived while I was speaking with the persons present. The paramedics treated the INJURED PERSON at the scene and he was than conveyed to the St Georges Hospital.

I attempted to ascertain how the INJURED PERSON had received his injury. I formed the opinion that the injury was not self-inflicted or accidental. I spoke with the three persons present and in view of their contradictory and inconsistent statements and the blood upon their persons I decided to arrest all three on suspicion of MALICIOUS WOUNDING OR ASSAULT OCCASIONING GRIEVOUS BODILY HARM.

I cautioned each suspect upon arrest and noted down the comments they made under caution.

>GEORGIA LANE
>TIME OF ARREST: 16:07
>COMMENT ON ARREST: What I'm his wife why are you arresting me

>ANNETTE MCALLISTER
>TIME OF ARREST: 16:11
>COMMENT ON ARREST: What are you talking about you must be kidding this is a domestic

>JACK MCALLISTER
>TIME OF ARREST: 16:14
>COMMENT ON ARREST: I don't get this why are you taking me it was Georgie that stabbed him

I arranged for all three DETAINED PERSONS to be conveyed to the CENTRAL POLICE STATION where they were booked into custody by PS 261 DAVID INGLETON.

Further officers then attended to secure the scene.

Nick then read through the individual custody records of each of the suspects: the detention reviews, the key times, the reasons for authorisation of detention. David had covered himself by calling out a doctor, who had turned up four hours later and simply written for each suspect: *Fit for detention. Fit for interview.* Nick knew that PC Lohan's description of glazed eyes and slurred speech was just the standard report wording of a bobby who spent most of his life arresting drunk people; the three suspects were probably only tipsy. There were no reports, comments, or notes from CID. They were aloof and self-contained, like a secret service or special agency. He didn't know DI Olding well; he knew her by sight and had spoken to her maybe half a dozen times. Usually it was only the more junior CID officers who came down to the cells to question suspects. He picked up the cordless telephone beside him, and then changed his mind and tapped out a message to DI Olding instead. *What's happening with the Riverside View GBH? I have three suspects in custody here, I need an update.* He paused, then deleted the second sentence and replaced it with: *Please let me have an update ASAP. Thanks.*

Katrina appeared at his elbow and slid a mug of tea on to the desk top.

"Thanks," said Nick. "That's just what I need." Katrina had both hands wrapped around her own mug, holding it close to her chest. "Are you okay?"

She pulled a face. "Yeah," she said.

"Really?"

She sighed. "I wasn't supposed to be working tonight. I'm not supposed to be working nights at all. I told them. No one else available, they said." She looked down at the steam of her tea. "I told them, I'm not doing nights any more, Stuart's in a lot of pain, I can't leave him on his own all night. Just this once, they said, but it's always just this once, isn't it?"

"Well," said Nick, awkwardly, "we're all grateful to you for coming in." He knew at once it was the wrong thing to say. It allied him to "them" - the management, the grinding machine, the faceless bosses - and Katrina looked away. He took a breath and tried to cover his mistake with a clumsy follow up. "How's Stuart doing?"

"He's in a lot of pain," she said, without looking at Nick.

The phone rang. Nick picked it up.

"Custody desk."

"Hi, this is DS Butland. You wanted an update on the GBH, yeah?" It sounded like he was using a mobile phone in a car, the background noise gushing and gurgling. "Yeah, we're still gathering evidence, right? We'll let you know when we're ready to interview."

"Okay…"

"The DI says we're not yet at the first review time, yeah? She says we'll have more info for you by the time of the eight hour review."

"Okay…"

DS Butland had already gone.

Nick put down the phone. A woman's voice had started shouting from the cells again. Katrina had slipped back into the kitchen.

"Um, Katrina?"

She re-appeared, hugging her mug.

"Could you go and check on the female prisoners now?"

"Yes, of course."

"Just a quick look in on them…" Katrina had already put down her mug and set off, tucking her hair behind her ears purposefully. He wondered if she was close to retirement yet; it was hard to tell her age. She might only be in her early fifties. A hard life could give a person that overused look. He was embarrassed that her knew so little about her; it was so easy to treat co-workers like part of the screwed-down furniture. "Thanks."

As she walked out, jangling keys, he remembered the PC in the corridor.

"Hey!" he called. "You can come through now."

2

Outside, it was night. Streetlamps streaked overhead as the unmarked car moved swiftly along the empty roads, too fast around the corners and uneven on the straights. DC Ehlen was driving; DS Butland, in the passenger seat with his knees and arms sprawled wide, looked at him sideways. "You ever been on a murder?" he asked.

DC Ehlen shook his head.

"This'll be a murder in less than an hour, I reckon. Did you see the photos? Fuck. He's had it. I bet we'll be wading in blood when we get there. Hope you've got a strong stomach."

DC Ehlen said nothing.

"Olding will be wetting herself on this one. Three suspects, all covered in blood, all blaming each other. Forensic won't tell us anything. No other witnesses. It's a nightmare, this one. I bet Olding's petrified. She could come out of this with three acquittals. She's right in the shit with this one."

DC Ehlen said nothing, but crunched the gears clumsily as they turned into Riverside View.

3

Aaron, a male custodian, had arrived on duty, and Nick asked him to take the new prisoner - a straightforward possession of cannabis - down to cell five. On his CCTV screen Nick could see an angle of corridor and Aaron walking past Katrina, who was locking a cell door on a shouting woman. Aaron was an odd man of indeterminate age, wearing large glasses and black hair combed into a crest. He was hard to connect with; casual conversation with him was like trying to grapple someone on ice skates. "Yes, Serge," he'd say, distantly.

"Biscuit?"

"No thanks, Serge."

The night shift was the biscuit shift. Nick had read somewhere that working nights made you eat too much - it messed up your hunger hormones or something. The staff canteen no longer opened at night but there were glowing machines upstairs dispensing crisps and chocolate and plastic cups of powdered soup. He had developed a taste for the tomato and basil; once rehydrated by the kettle it was bright red and greasy with green flecks floating in it and a sharp, wake-up taste, like salty coffee. He could almost feel his blood pressure rising as he drank it.

Katrina came back from the cells.

"Biscuit?"

She took one and thoughtfully bit into it. "I think you're going to have to talk to that woman in cell one," she said.

"Georgia Lane?"

Katrina nodded. "She's hysterical. She says she's thrown up twice. I can't calm her down. She says she needs to speak to the person in charge."

Nick nodded grimly and brushed the biscuit crumbs from his hands. He followed Katrina down the corridor to cell one.

The corridor was well scrubbed and lit by overhead fluorescent lights in cages. Each numbered cell door was a heavy slab of metal with a sliding hatch, behind which was a grille at face height. Katrina had her keys on a long looping chain attached to her belt. She checked through the hatch and then opened the door.

The windowless cell, like all the cells, was a small square space containing a metal toilet bowl and a bed with a thin plastic mattress. It smelled bad. In this cell there was a woman sitting on the bed. She jumped up as they walked in.

"I'm Sergeant Nick Toft," said Nick. "I'm the custody sergeant."

Georgia Lane was a tall, long-boned woman, with a large jaw. Her hair, streaked in expensive shades of blond, was knotted back. She had been crying, but her makeup had put up a fight, and held firm. She was wearing gold-trimmed sandals and a white paper suit.

The white paper suits were zip-up one-pieces given to suspects whose clothes were seized for forensic examination. They were one-size-fits-all, elasticated at the wrists and ankles, and cheaply made; not strictly paper, their fabric was thin and waxy, with the look and feel of paper food packaging. In theory they were opaque, but sometimes black or brightly coloured underwear showed through. It was unusual for a detained person to be put in a paper suit: it meant they had been brought in for a serious offence, and so within the custody area they were treated with particular care and deference.

Georgia Lane was also wearing a grey blanket over her shoulders, as if she was a victim of an apocalyptic natural disaster, and she kept the blanket around her as she looked at Nick. "Are you in charge?" she demanded.

"Yes, I'm - "

"Why am I here?"

"You've been arrested on suspicion of assault occasioning grievous bod - "

"Don't give me all that crap again! Are you a robot or something? My husband's been stabbed, my husband!" She lifted her chin. "He's in hospital, he could die - I should be with him!"

Nick nodded. "I understand why you're distressed…"

"Look at me! I mean, look at me! Why are you doing this to me?"

"… but the assault on your husband has to be properly investigated, and the officers in the case need to detain you…"

"Are you human?"

"… for questioning. There are enquiries that need to be made…"

"He could die!"

"… so the officers can understand what has happened…"

"I've been here for hours!" She was choking on her words now and starting to cry, her face turning red as her composure drained away. She was clenching the edges of the grey blanket with ring-encrusted hands and long silver-painted nails.

"I'm sorry," Nick said. "But we have to investigate this matter properly. I will get on to the CID officers to expedite the matter."

"You're all mad," she said, and sat down abruptly on the edge of the bed.

Nick was looking at her rings. They were oversized, set with large stones, like a row of knuckledusters across her fists. David should have taken them off her.

"Um," Nick said, "I'm afraid I'm going to have to ask you to remove your rings."

"You what?"

"Your rings. It's my duty to remove anything that could be used to harm yourself or others…"

"You're kidding me!"

"They'll be kept safely and you can have them back when you leave." He was looking at her nails, too, which were like talons, curved and shiny and painted in speckled silver. Nick wondered if they were real. If they were false, they would presumably break off easily; but if they were real, he couldn't ask her to remove them…

"You're evil!"

"My priority is the safety of - "

"My husband's dying and you want to take off my fucking rings? Are you fucking OCD or something?"

"I just need you to remove them…"

"They won't come off! So fuck you!"

And then she started screaming.

Just screaming. Her face was red, her mouth was open, and she was staring at him, like a defiant toddler. Nick held up his palms. "Mrs Lane, you're not doing yourself any good carrying on like that." He would have to give up on the rings. He'd make a note on the custody record that they couldn't be removed. "I will contact CID now and do everything I can to get this case moved on quickly."

She wasn't listening; in fact, Nick could hardly hear himself. He and Katrina retreated from the room and locked the door.

There was another woman's voice, shouting from cell ten.

"That's the other one," sighed Katrina. She slid back the hatch and raised her voice. "Calm down, Annette, calm down."

"Is that Georgie screaming?"

"Yes."

"I want to make a statement."

"Someone will come to interview you in - "

"I've got important information. Evidence. It wasn't Georgie that did it. I need to talk to someone."

"Soon." Katrina slid the hatch back, muffling the woman's voice.

"I'll get on to CID," said Nick.

"They always take ages." Katrina sounded resigned.

Back at the desk, Aaron was squinting at the computer screen and picking his nose. Nick took up the phone and dialled DI Olding. He half expected it to go straight to messages.

"Olding."

"Oh, hi, this is Sergeant Toft, down in custody. I need to know what's happening with this GBH."

"We're still making enquiries."

"I've got a woman here who's been in custody for six hours while her husband's in a critical state in hospital," Nick said. "She's in great distress."

There was a pause.

"Well," said Inspector Olding, reasonably, "she is the main suspect in her husband's stabbing."

"Have you got a statement from him?"

"He's not fit to make a statement."

There was another pause.

"Look," said Inspector Olding. "We're nearly ready to do the interviews, and we'll question her first, okay? Give us another twenty minutes."

"Okay."

"Has she asked for a solicitor?"

"Uh… yes, she has."

"You'd better get the solicitor here then."

"Will do," said Nick, and rang off.

"That bloke says it was an accident," said Aaron.

"Huh?"

Aaron was leaning with his elbows on the desk contemplatively. "That bloke in cell four. Jack McAllister. I took him a cup of tea. He says that the bloke fell on the knife." He scratched his ear. "He says it's all a big mistake, like."

Nick thought for a moment. "Have you made a note of this on the custody record?"

Aaron looked at him.

"It could be important. It could be a murder case, this one. We need to let CID know everything the suspects say."

Aaron continued to scratch his ear, and Nick began to tap purposefully at the computer keyboard.

4

Detective Inspector Rose Olding hated the CID office at night. Not that it was particularly welcoming in daylight. The police station was a grey pebbledash 1960s building, punctuated with small square windows made even smaller when the old metal frames were replaced with thick white plastic. Even during the day the fluorescent lights had to be left on. At night, the artificial light took over the whole space like a creeping infection, yellow light on yellow walls making Rose's eyes burn.

The CID office was open plan, under a low soft-tiled ceiling, the desks arranged awkwardly amongst random half-height wall dividers. The computers and printers emanated a background sense of electrical radiation and Rose always felt that she had a headache coming on. At night the windows were closed off with thin metallic blinds, horizontal strips so flimsy that if you parted them to look out they would flip and crease and get tangled in one another. They made a weak, tinny sound when jostled.

The cleaners came out at night, and as Rose's team sat around a central desk on uncomfortable swivel chairs a woman in an overall came wandering through the room, slowly dragging a noisy pink vacuum cleaner. Its painted face grinned at them. Rose's mother would have said that all the electromagnetism in the room would give them all cancer by the age of forty.

Rose herself was less than a year away from forty, and the rest of her team seemed to her to be unfeasibly young and energetic. DC Sophie Frank, barely twenty-five, perfectly groomed, quick. DS Hal Petersen, thirty, perfectly groomed, quick. Rose had sent Butland and Ehlen to visit the crime scene: the uniformed officers hadn't provided her with any descriptions or photographs, and forensics would take forever. At the moment all she had to go on was the initial arresting officer and the comments of a pessimistic doctor.

"So," she summed up, "we're expecting the McAllisters to blame the wife, but we don't know yet what the wife will say."

"We could question the McAllisters first," proposed Sophie. "Then we'll have clear allegations to put to the wife."

"If they saw her do it," agreed Hal, "it's easy: we charge her and take statements from them."

"Maybe." Rose was circumspect. "The problem is, when I spoke to the arresting officer it was clear that their verbals at the scene were a lot more confused. He said the wife was blaming the McAllisters; there was a reason why he arrested all three of them."

"He just didn't put it in his report," pointed out Hal.

"It's not exactly comprehensive," grinned Sophie. She put on a gruff, uniformed-sergeant voice. " 'I attended the scene and arrested everyone in sight'."

"I'm inclined to interview the wife first," said Rose. She didn't say so, but she felt uncomfortable about the wife's situation. This was a woman who could be innocent, whose husband was in hospital barely clinging to life, and Rose was about to put her through more trauma by interrogating her, and keeping her in a bleak cell, away from what could be her husband's last hours. Rose tapped on the desk, thinking. She knew that the forensic evidence, when it eventually came, would most likely be useless, since all three suspects had been at the scene: this case was all about questioning, and the questioning would be like flailing around in the dark. It wasn't a scripted TV drama, where a killer question could fire like a magic bullet and solve the case. Everyone lies. Rose knew that. Even innocent people lie. There was no guarantee they would ever find out what happened.

Rose sighed. "If only they could invent a lie detector that works."

Hal laughed. "I'd love a mind reading device."

"Recording devices in everyone's brain," added Sophie. "Just playback to get all the answers."

"CCTV cameras in every street. In every home."

"A full DNA database, at least."

"Satellites that see everything."

"Satellites with x-ray cameras."

Rose was smiling. "Until then," she said, "I guess we'll just have to be clever."

"We can do clever," said Sophie.

Rose slapped the desk decisively. "We'll interview the wife first. You and me, Hal."

"I'll sketch out some questions." Hal set to work, eager as a ferret. "We'll pin her down to timings, background, who came to the house that day…"

"There's an email from Butland," Sophie announced, looking at the monitor on the desk. "He's sending photos of the kitchen… ooh and a sketch of the house layout, that'll be useful. I'll print all this out for you."

Rose was nodding when her phone rang.

"Olding."

"Custody here. Jack McAllister's solicitor has arrived. I wondered if you wanted to go with him first."

"I thought we were doing the wife first?"

"Her solicitor's delayed. About an hour."

Rose drummed her fingers on the desk.

"Something else you should know," added the custody sergeant.

"What?"

"This Jack McAllister said something to one of my custody staff. It wasn't under caution, but I've noted it down. He says the victim fell on the knife. He's saying it was an accident."

"That's pretty unlikely."

"Yes, but I thought you should know."

Rose paused. It might make sense to question McAllister first if he was going to come up with a ridiculous story. It was always good to get obvious lies on record. "Okay. We'll start with him." She rang off. "We're doing Jack McAllister first."

"But we said…"

"Change of plan."

5

Nick had charged and bailed the drunk driver in cell six but almost at once a new guest had been brought in: a rather more complicated drunk in charge. A well-dressed, well-spoken man in his sixties, he had been found in his car parked up at the side of the road by two PCs who were finding him very amusing. Nick could see why: the man was clearly very drunk, but desperately pretending to be sober. He walked very deliberately from the door to the desk in a graceful curve, and then stood swaying gently like a sapling in a breeze, his chin held high in what was intended to be a dignified expression. He gave his name, very carefully, as Brian Christopher Dunn.

"Date of birth?"

"Excusem, excuse me?"

"What's your date of birth?"

"Um… July. The twenty-seventh day of July."

"What year?"

"Excusem?"

Nick moved patiently through his procedures while the two constables sniggered. They knew it would be hard to prove he'd been driving, so they wanted to interview him in the hope of getting an admission.

"Breathalyse him now," Nick told them, "and then we'll put him in a cell until he's sobered up enough for interview. You might be waiting until lunchtime tomorrow though."

Dunn was dismayed when he cottoned on to the fact that he was going in a cell.

"I need you to remove your tie and your belt," Nick said. He had to repeat himself several times before Dunn understood. "It's procedure, sir."

"Pro… pro…" Dunn was wide eyed. "D'ye think I'd hang myself?"

"It's just procedure, sir. I have to make sure you're safe." He turned to Aaron, who was chewing a pen. "I think we'll have checks on Mr Dunn every twenty minutes for now."

In the meantime the CID officers had turned up and taken Jack McAllister into an interview room, so Nick took the opportunity to slip out of the back door for a quick cigarette. It was a warm night. The car park was lit by oversized, overbright lights on stalks, almost like stadium lights, blocking out the stars. The cars seemed to huddle close to the ground. Nick leaned against the wall, holding the door open with his boot, and savoured the moment of cigarette and solitude. The pebbledash wall was coarse and scratchy through his sleeve.

He pulled out his phone and sent a text to his son. *Look like the innocent flower, but be the serpent under it*. They had laughed over that quote from *Macbeth* because Nick had said the custody suite was full of innocent flowers. It had been a special afternoon, just him and Joe hanging out together, talking about Joe's exams; Nick had made bacon sandwiches and Joe had said that his mother was driving him crazy. "I swear she's more uptight about my exams than I am," he said. It was a new experience for Nick to be the superior parent. Since the divorce, six years ago, Nick had believed that his deficiencies as a father had contributed to his deficiencies as a husband, and at first it had been difficult to even maintain contact with the kids. His shift work didn't fit with being a weekend father. His ex-wife, Ellie, treated him to an exaggerated exasperated performance every time he tried to re-arrange a visit, and the children themselves were busy with friends and clubs; he thought that by their teenage years he would have lost them. But he had persisted: and now here was Joe, dropping round on a Sunday afternoon with *Macbeth* and a maths workbook. "I can't revise with Mum around," he declared. "Honestly, she can't leave me alone. She makes me second guess myself."

It was never too late to make a fresh start. It had taken Nick years to realise that. Life was continually changing, and the change wasn't just in one direction. When his marriage went into decline he started to see life as a process of entropy, a steady dissolution, love seeping away and hair falling out and fitness levels falling. He would gradually become older and slower and more and more forgetful, and nothing new would ever happen to him. It was a revelation to find that his relationship with Joe had taken an upswing; his daughter Lucy, too, had become more friendly as she grew up. "Why aren't you dating, Dad?" she asked him on his birthday, adding, with a grin, "Maybe you need to lose some of that belly."

He finished his cigarette and stubbed it out on the wall. It was against the rules to hold the back door open, but he would feel a fool if he was locked out of his own custody suite, pressing the bell to be buzzed back in. He needed to be there, supervising, at all times. He pulled the heavy door wide and went back inside, just as Georgia Lane started up again, shouting hoarsely.

6

The interview room was small, windowless, and painted in an indecisive shade of blue-grey. There was a wooden table with wooden benches either side, a clock on the wall, and a camera in the corner. Rose arranged Jack McAllister and his solicitor on one side of the table and herself and Hal on the other.

"This is all a mistake," Jack was saying as they sat down.

"That's okay," Rose said, nodding. "You'll get a chance to tell us everything, just wait for us to get properly started."

The solicitor was Sam Stead; Rose had met him a few times before and found him quite reasonable. He wasn't a proper solicitor but rather a trained-up legal clerk; nowadays you rarely saw fully qualified solicitors in the police station because the work was so poorly paid. Sam looked sleepy and a bit crumpled, in his weekend clothes, a bright t-shirt and sagging trousers. Rose and Hal, in suits, were the smart side of the table. Jack was wearing a white paper one-piece.

"You do the honours," Rose said to Hal. They both set out their folders and clicked their pens, and a sense of anticipation hung in the room. Sam Stead blew his nose.

"Right, the time is... twenty-two fifty-one, and this is an interview at Central Police Station with Jack McAllister," Hal announced. "Can I just check with you, Jack, your date of birth is...?

"Twentieth of May 1985," said Jack. "Look, I need to tell you that this is all a terrible accident…"

"Just let me get the formalities out of the way, please," said Hal smoothly. "Your address is 9 Riverside View, yes?"

"Yes."

"And your occupation?"

"I'm a Project Manager at Systems Solutions."

"That's great Jack, thank you. Also present are Detective Inspector Olding, myself - Detective Sergeant Petersen - and your legal representative, Samuel Smith. Now, Jack, I have to remind you that you are under caution. You do not have to say anything, but it may harm your defence if you do not mention when questioned something which you later rely on in court. Anything you do say may be used in evidence. Do you understand?"

"Yes, look, I know this looks bad," started Jack, "but this was actually an accident. Carl was using this knife, right, a big, you know, kitchen knife, and he was chopping lemons, you know, for the drinks - we were having cocktails - and he fell… I know it sounds weird, but that's what happened. He was holding the knife in his hand and he slipped and fell on it and it went, you know, into his neck."

Hal and Rose and Sam were all scribbling rapidly, noting down this initial statement. All three of them were thinking this would come back to bite him. Jack himself looked earnest, and emphatic, gesturing with his hands as he spoke and sitting forward with his white-clad elbows on the table. He was a slim man with short, smooth-combed hair and a close-trimmed beard; he had a big nose, and the rest of his face arranged itself around it. He finished speaking and swallowed nervously.

"Okay," said Rose. "Thanks for that, Jack. I'd just like to take you back a little bit. We're talking about an incident that took place today at 6 Riverside View, aren't we? Can you tell me who lives there?"

"Carl and Georgia."

"Carl and Georgia Lane. And you live at number 9 with…"

"Annette. My wife."

"Your wife. Is it just the two of you? Any kids?"

"No. Actually we've been trying. Been trying for about a year now."

"Okay. So can you tell me how well you and your wife know your neighbours, the Lanes?"

"Um, well, you know, we see them quite a bit. We've been living there two, three years, and they moved in just after us. We, you know, go round for dinner, drinks, New Year, that kind of thing."

"And what are they like?"

"Oh, um, well, they're nice, you know, we get on well."

"How would you describe them?"

"Well, I suppose they're… quite a cool couple, you know?" He shrugged. "Fashionable. Popular. Fun."

"Do they have children?"

"No."

"Do they get on well with each other?"

"Um, well, I suppose so. You never really know, do you?"

Rose nodded. "So, let's talk about today. You and your wife went round to their house."

"Yeah, it was a barbecue. The weather's turned really nice and Georgie said, you know, come round for a barbie."

"Right. What time did you and Annette go round there?"

"Um, it was two o'clock. We were going to have a few drinks and then fire up the barbecue later on, you know?"

"So, you and your wife arrived there at two o'clock. Who was there when you arrived?"

"Just Carl and Georgia."

"Was anyone else invited?"

"No."

"So, you arrived at two; did you go into their garden, or…?"

"Yeah, it was a lovely day, so we all sat in the garden."

"Did you have a drink?"

"Yeah, Georgie was making these cocktails. I don't know what was in them. I had two or three, got a bit merry, you know."

"Who else was drinking cocktails?"

"We all were."

"And how were you all getting along?"

"Oh, great, fine."

"Were there any arguments?"

"No, no."

"Any raised voices?"

"No."

"Any arguments between Carl and Georgia? Any tension between them?"

"No, no."

"Did anyone else come to the house?"

"No."

"Or into the garden?"

"No."

"Did Georgia go into the kitchen to make the cocktails?"

"Yes."

"Did you go into the house?"

"Um, well, you know, when Carl got hurt."

"Okay. I want to take you to the moment when Carl got hurt."

"Okay."

"Now you said that everyone was in the garden; so how did Carl come to be in the kitchen?"

"He went in to get more drinks. Or, you know, the ingredients for drinks, I don't know."

"Okay. Before that moment, had *you* been in the kitchen?"

"Well, you know, you have to go through the kitchen to get to the garden."

Rose nodded. "I see. So, was that the only time you had been in the kitchen? When you walked through to get to the garden?"

"Yes."

"You didn't make any drinks in the kitchen?"

"No."

"Prepared any food?"

"No."

"Touched any utensils? Any knives?"

"Oh. No."

"Had you chopped any lemons or anything?"

"No."

"Okay. So, from when you walked through the kitchen to go into the garden, up until when Carl got hurt, during that time had you come back into the house at all?"

"No."

"Had Annette?"

"Um, no."

"Okay. Now tell me exactly what happened when Carl got hurt."

"Well, he was cutting up lemons, you know, to go in the drinks, and he was using this really big knife, and he was holding it like this, and you know, not paying much attention - he'd had a few drinks by then - and then he kind of slipped, like this." Jack bobbed his head and shoulders forward, holding his fist at chest height, as if falling on to it. "And the knife - it was really sharp, you know those kitchen knives - it went in his neck."

"Okay. And you saw this happen?"

"Um, no."

"You didn't see this happen?"

"No. I wasn't there."

"So how do you know what happened?"

"Um, someone told me."

"Jack, you're going to have to be a bit clearer about this."

"Um, I suppose it was Georgia that told me. We were in the garden, you know, and then Georgie went into the kitchen and she started screaming, and so we ran in and there was Carl, lying on the floor with the knife in his neck. There was all this blood everywhere and Georgie was panicking."

"Jack, a few minutes ago you mimed what happened to Carl, do you remember? You said he fell like this…"

"Yeah."

"But now you're saying you didn't see that at all."

"Yes. Sorry. It was Georgie told me that was what happened. It was all confusing... Carl was bleeding so much, and we were trying to help him." Jack looked down at his hands, which emerged, clean, from the rough elasticated cuffs of the white suit. "I wrapped a tea towel round his neck. I knew not to pull the knife out, so I sort of wrapped it... there was blood everywhere, all over my clothes and my hands. It was horrible." He paused. "Is, is Carl going to be okay?"

"We don't know yet," Rose explained. "He's at the hospital and they're doing what they can."

"Yeah."

"Jack. Did you call the ambulance?"

"Yeah. No, Annette did, on her mobile, I remember that."

"Where were you?"

"I, you know, I stayed with Carl."

"Okay. Do you remember the police arriving?"

"Yes."

"There was a police officer, PC Lohan - he's a smallish chap, grey hair, glasses - do you remember him? He was the one who arrested you."

"Uh, yeah."

"You remember him?"

"Yes."

"Now, when he arrested you, he cautioned you, just as Hal did just now; he said you didn't have to say anything but anything you did say could be used in evidence... do you remember him arresting you?"

"Uh, yeah."

"Now, he wrote down what you said when he arrested you." Rose could remember the words, but she pulled the arrest report out of her file. "Here's what you said." She read from the printed sheet. " 'I don't get this why are you taking me it was Georgie that stabbed him.' " She looked up at Jack questioningly.

There was a pause, and Jack sat back from the table, took a breath, and then leaned forward again.

"Well," he said. "Well. I... well, I was quite upset then you know... and, yeah, well, I suppose at that time I did think that Georgia had stabbed him. Yeah."

"So," said Rose carefully, "at the time when PC Lohan arrested you, at that time, you thought Georgia had stabbed Carl?"

"Yes."

"So what happened to change your mind?"

"Well, Georgie told me it was an accident."

Rose nodded. "So, when did she tell you this?"

"I don't know."

"You don't know."

"Look..." Jack held up his hands. "Look, I don't know what happened. I was in the garden, with Annette, it was a lovely day, we were all chatting and having a drink, and then the next thing, there's Georgie screaming and Carl's been stabbed. I don't want to say she did it - I didn't see her do it, I didn't see it happen. I just don't know, I don't know what happened. I know I didn't stab him, I know Annette didn't stab him... him and Georgia were in the kitchen together and I don't know what happened."

"Okay," said Rose. She tucked her paperwork back into her file and settled her hands across it, fingers interlaced. "We'll leave it there for now. Obviously we'll be questioning the others to see what they say." She paused delicately. "And we will need to speak to you again when we get a statement from Carl."

Jack didn't respond at first, then slowly looked up. "Oh, right, is he, you know, is he okay enough to do that?"

"We're just waiting for that information."

"Oh. Okay."

"So we will need to speak to you again." Rose turned to Hal. "Was there anything else?"

Hal looked thoughtful. "Jack, what would you say if I was to tell you your fingerprints were found on the knife?"

Sam Stead jumped straight in. "Are you saying his fingerprints *have* been found on the knife?"

Hal licked his lips. "We don't actually have that evidence back yet; I was just…"

"But I did touch the knife," Jack interrupted. "I was trying to stop the blood, you know, with the tea towel - I probably did touch the knife. I was trying to save his life."

Hal nodded. "Okay."

"I was trying to save his life," Jack repeated, his voice breaking. It seemed that the enormity of it all had caught up with him, and he put his face in his hands. Rose wrapped up the formalities of the interview.

"Can I see Annette?" Jack asked, quietly. When he took his hands away his face was wet and blotchy. He sniffed and rubbed his nose.

"Not yet," Rose explained. "We can't let you speak to each other until you've both been interviewed."

They all stood up. Jack nodded and wiped his face on the sleeve of his paper suit, as Hal opened the door to usher him out.

7

Nick was booking in another detainee, a regular called Alan Stamper, who had been dragged in for assaulting his wife. Alan was toothless and wild-haired and smelled of stale beer. He was stabbing the air with his bony finger. "This is bullshit," he repeated. "This is a stitch up."

"Calm down, Alan," said Nick. The arresting officer, PC Lasky, had put on blue vinyl gloves to do a pat down search, but he was struggling because Alan was so agitated, jerking forward as he spoke, waving his arms, and glaring at Nick. He was in his late fifties but tall and wiry, a man who had done manual work all his life and had convictions going back forty years.

"ABH? That's bullshit. ABH?" ABH meant assault occasioning actual bodily harm.

"She had a split lip, Alan," said PC Lasky, wearily.

"You call that ABH? Did you see what she done to me? You see this?" He hoisted up his t-shirt, revealing brown-blotched skin and wrinkled scars. "You see this? She stabbed me, right there." It was an old scar. "And here" - he was trying to twist round to show them the back of his shoulder - "she hit me with a bloody spade, there."

"I know, Alan, I know," said PC Lasky. "But none of that happened today, did it? We're just looking at what's gone on today."

"This is bullshit!"

"Calm down, Alan," said Nick, "and we can get all of this sorted." He could see the CID officers hovering in the doorway and he sent Aaron to return Jack McAllister to his cell. "Then you can come back for Alan," he added.

"This - is - bull - shit," shouted Alan, spraying spit and pointing emphatically on each syllable.

"Just stay calm and we'll get it sorted out," repeated Nick. "Cell three," he told Aaron.

"Bullshit!"

Once Alan had been safely stowed away, PC Lasky ripped off the vinyl gloves and leaned on the desk. "I'm going to give her a couple of hours to sober up before I take a statement off her," he said. "To be honest, I reckon she'll have decided to drop the complaint and have him back by then."

"Fair enough," said Nick. His latest cup of tea had gone cold. PC Lasky tossed his gloves at the bin.

"Right then, " he said. "Guess I'd better get back out there."

8

"I don't know if that went well or not," said Hal. They were back in the CID office. The cleaner had gone, and the room seemed large and quiet, as if everyone else in the building had gone home. Rose could hear the fluorescent lights buzzing.

"It depends what the others come out with," she said. "Are these all the photos Butland took?"

Sophie nodded. Rose had spread the pictures out in a row across the desk. There were six, all taken in the kitchen. Butland had taken them quickly, on his phone, and they were awkward, thin pictures, from strange angles, like snaps taken at a party, or stills from a disorientating horror movie. There was a glimpse of a granite worktop and half a lemon on a chopping board; there were splashes of blood on kitchen cupboards; there was a dark stain that might have been blood on slate flooring. It was impossible to put them together to form the shape of a room or to get any sense of layout or proportions. Rose sighed. There was poignancy in the background details - a pink kettle, grinning photos on the fridge - ordinary, everyday things from ordinary, everyday lives, which made the splattered blood look more grotesque.

"We should have shown McAllister these," said Rose. "We should have got him to describe exactly where Carl and Georgia were when he went into the kitchen."

Rose had a tendency to beat herself up in this way, to think of all the things she should have done after the opportunity had passed. Her ex-husband, Gavin, used to say, "Stop looking backwards: you can't change anything now." He approached life with an unapologetic confidence; self-criticism was unknown to him. A lot of people found him arrogant. Rose found him arrogant. "Never mind," she said.

"I didn't get very far with the fingerprints on the knife," said Hal.

"Have they got fingerprints off the knife?" asked Sophie, in surprise.

"No, I was bluffing," explained Hal. "I imagine the knife's still in the chap's neck. Or on some dish at the hospital covered in the prints of half a dozen medics."

"They wear gloves," said Sophie, hopefully. "We might get some prints."

Rose gathered up the photos. "We'd better get down there and interview the wife. Isn't Butland back yet?"

"No," said Sophie, "he's taking statements from some of the neighbours."

Rose looked up.

"Nothing very useful," Sophie clarified. "No-one saw or heard anything; it's just some background info."

"Gossip," grinned Hal.

"Yep."

"Right," said Rose. "Okay, follow ups… Sophie, find out whether McAllister was brought in in the same car as Georgia, whether they had a chance to talk to each other… in fact, get hold of PC Lohan and tell him I want a full statement from him, everything he heard the suspects say, to him or to each other, everything. And get on to Forensics and tell them we need a preliminary report." She picked up her folder and phone. "We'll go down to the cells and interview Georgia Lane." She stood up. "I'm not looking forward to this."

9

Georgia Lane sat in the interview room with the grey blanket over her hunched shoulders, like the shawl of a wise woman, and her arms on the table, leaning so far forward that Rose and Hal had to shuffle their folders back into their laps. Her hands, glittery with gold and silver, looked like someone else's hands, thrusting unreasonably out of her white paper sleeves. Her eyes were bloodshot and wild, and her voice, hoarse from screaming, wobbled like a crooked wheel on a cart, sometimes barking and sometimes squeaking. "It was just a barbecue," she was saying. "Just, you know, a nice day, a Sunday, so we had a barbecue." She shrugged.

"And you invited Jack and Annette McAllister?"

"Yeah."

"Anyone else?"

"No. It was just a spontaneous thing."

Rose nodded. "Tell me about the McAllisters. What are they like?"

Georgia shrugged again. The whole blanket lifted as she moved, making her presence large in the room. Her solicitor, a small young woman beside her, was perched on the very end of the bench.

"They're okay; they're just neighbours, yeah? Ordinary people, a bit dull really. She's weird though. She's unhappy, angry, uptight. Like a coiled spring. She hits Jack. I reckon she did it - she's the one who stabbed Carl. She seems all little and mousey, but she's got a temper. She can snap over nothing."

"Okay," said Rose, carefully. "Let me ask you a few questions about yourself. You and Carl, how long have you been married?"

"Three years."

"Any kids?"

"No."

"And you said you're a personal trainer; where do you work?"

"First For Fitness."

"And what does Carl do?"

"Carl? He runs his own business. Fine Grooves."

"What's that?"

Georgia looked at them. "Fine Grooves, yeah? Most people have heard of it. He sells rare and collectable vinyl. He sells all over the world - there was a whole piece about him in the local paper."

Rose nodded.

"It's a very successful business. Over a hundred thousand turnover in the first year. He has a global reputation."

"Okay," said Rose. "So, tell me what happened today."

"Well, we were all in the garden, drinking, hanging out, all getting on fine, yeah? I mean, people get a bit tetchy in hot weather after a few drinks, but everything was fine... and I went in to the loo, upstairs, and when I came down they were all in the kitchen, and Carl had been stabbed. It was all..." She raised her hands in a helpless gesture. "Unbelievable."

"So when you went off to the loo they were all still in the garden?"

"Yes."

"And how long were you in the loo?"

"I don't know… I was a while because I went to brush out my hair and tie it back, because it was such a warm day, and I fixed up my makeup too. I went into the bedroom as well as the bathroom. I went to the loo, washed my hands, then into the bedroom to brush out my hair, tie it back, fix up my makeup… Maybe five minutes?"

"Okay, about five minutes. Did you hear any raised voices?"

"Honestly? I don't know. I wasn't listening out, you know?"

"Did you shut the kitchen door behind you when you went upstairs?"

"I have no idea."

"Okay. Tell me exactly what you saw when you went into the kitchen."

"Well, I saw Carl… fucking hell, he was on the floor with a knife in his neck. It was horrible. There was blood just gushing out… and Jack and Annette were both there, and everyone just seemed to be shouting. It was horrible. Unbelievable."

"So you didn't see what happened?"

"No I didn't. But I reckon it was her. She's like Jekyll and Hyde. I've seen her lose her temper before."

"When?"

"With Jack. Quite a few times… the worst, though, that was a few months back, around Valentine's. They invited us round for a meal, yeah? She had a bottle of wine or two and she just suddenly lost it with Jack, completely out of the blue, going on about how he wasn't serious about her, how he didn't want kids…" Georgia shook her head. "It was mental. She really flew at him. I mean, she was hitting him, like punches, on the arm; he was holding his arms up to defend himself, like this. It was embarrassing. We went home."

"Did she cause him injury?"

"I don't know - we left while they were still at it. Jack was embarrassed afterwards, but she just pretended like nothing had happened. Maybe she didn't even know she'd done it."

"Were there any arguments today?"

"No, I don't think so."

"You're not sure?"

"No, I don't remember any arguments."

"Between Jack and Annette?"

"No."

"Between you and Carl?"

"No, not at all. We don't argue. Look, I didn't stab him. I know what you think. I love him, we're really happy. I don't know what you've been hearing, but it's rubbish."

"What do you think we've been hearing?"

"I don't know. You tell me. That lot in Riverside View are all nutters."

"Do you think…"

"Jealous, that's what they are - they're all jealous because of Carl, because he's so successful. They don't like it."

"Okay. Can I ask…"

"They've tried to report him to the council for running a business from home. He doesn't - he's got a lock up, but he keeps the most valuable records at the house for security, that's all. Some of those records are worth two or three hundred."

"Okay…"

"Jealous. They're all pathetic. Pathetic, little lives... Jack and Annette too, they're jealous." Her angry gestures nearly made the blanket slide off her shoulders, and she snatched at it. "They're pathetic."

Rose nodded. "Okay. Can I ask you about the knife?"

Georgia tugged the blanket around her, holding it at her throat. "It was a big kitchen knife. I was using it to slice lemons, for the drinks. I bet her fingerprints are on it. It was just on the side, on a chopping board - she could have grabbed it. Are her prints on it?"

"We don't know yet," said Rose.

"I bet they are."

"You didn't actually see it happen, did you?"

"No, but it was one of them, her or him. They were the only people there."

"It could have been an accident," said Hal.

"An accident? How do you accidentally get stabbed?"

Georgia suddenly started crying. The grey blanket heaved up and down and she buried her face in her hands on the table.

Rose paused.

"Georgia, I have just one more question."

Georgia was sobbing.

"Did you tell Jack it was an accident?"

"I think we should take a break there," said the solicitor. "My client's in understandable distress."

Rose nodded. "Okay, we'll stop there for now. The time is... exactly half past midnight, and I'm bringing this interview to a close."

10

Georgia Lane was taken back to her cell by Katrina, but her solicitor wanted to make representations to the custody sergeant. She was a very young woman, probably a clerk or a trainee, and she was very small and dainty. Standing in front of the big custody desk, clutching her tablet computer against her cardigan, she looked to Rose like a schoolgirl.

"I'd like to make representations," she said to Nick.

Nick nodded and rested his substantial forearms, crossed, on top of the desk. "Go ahead."

"I'd like to argue that my client should be released on bail," she began. "Her husband is in hospital in a critical condition. It's possible that he might not survive. You could bail her to come back tomorrow morning, so she could go to the hospital now to be with him. She has a fixed address - she's a homeowner - and she has no previous convictions. There's no reason to believe she won't answer her bail. She's already been interviewed in relation to this matter. She's answered all questions put to her. There's no longer any reason to keep her here."

Nick nodded. "Inspector?"

"I understand that this is a distressing situation," said Rose, "but there is good evidence for Georgia to be held on suspicion of assaulting her husband, and I would definitely object to her being released on bail at this time. If she were to attend the hospital and speak to her husband now, she could influence any statement he might make, and she might even be a danger to him. She could also interfere with evidence back at the crime scene. This enquiry is still in its early stages: forensic evidence is still being gathered and we still have a further suspect to interview, and other possible witnesses to speak to in the neighbouring houses."

Nick nodded. "I've heard your representations, and I will note them down on the custody record, but at this stage I don't think bail is appropriate because of the danger that your client will interfere with witnesses or interfere with evidence. I'm authorising her continued detention at this time."

The solicitor nodded.

"I'll buzz you out," said Nick.

"We'll ring you when we need to speak to her again," said Rose.

The solicitor said goodbye and headed to the back door. Nick watched her go into the corridor on his monitor, and then pressed the door release button. Rose checked her phone.

"Biscuit?" said Nick.

Rose laughed. "Have you got a range of snacks squirrelled away back there?"

"That's about right," said Nick.

Rose took a biscuit. Hal had gone back to the CID office and Aaron was in the little kitchen, boiling the kettle. The custody area was momentarily peaceful.

"So do you think the wife did it?" asked Nick.

Rose sighed. "I wish I knew."

"It's a tricky one."

"At least he's still alive."

"Do you think he'll pull through?"

"I don't know. From the initial report, I thought this would definitely turn into a murder, but he's hanging in there. With each hour that passes his chances improve."

"And if he survives, he can tell you what happened."

"That's what I'm hoping." Rose took another biscuit.

"You've still got the McAllister woman to interview."

"I know. What will she say? Aliens did it?"

Nick laughed and wiped the crumbs from his mouth. "Do you want a cup of tea?"

Rose shook her head. "I have to get back up to the office."

"Ah, back up above ground level. Must be lovely."

Rose laughed. "I wouldn't say that."

"I know," grinned Nick, "you envy us down here, in our cosy underground den."

"Well, you have biscuits and a kettle."

"What more does anyone need?"

Rose picked up her things and went out, smiling. "See you later."

11

Annette McAllister was small and dark-eyed, her hair a brunette bob and her eyebrows painted in thick bands like an Egyptian queen. Her mascara was clotted and she had chewed off her lipstick. Her nails were painted turquoise and her thin hands looked pale and bloodless; she sat twisting her wedding ring round and round. The white paper suit puffed out around her, far too large, as if she had been bundled into an enormous bag.

"Yes, that's right," she said. She had listened very carefully as Hal asked her to confirm her date of birth and address, and she now answered him very seriously, as intensely focussed as someone taking an oral exam. She had declined a solicitor.

"And what's your occupation?"

"I work at Asda," she said, twisting her wedding ring.

"And you live with your husband, Jack McAllister?"

"Yes."

"Any children?"

"No."

Her eyes were fixed on Hal's face, and she answered every question solemnly. Unlike Jack and Georgia, she wasn't in a rush to volunteer information, and Rose wondered if that meant she was hiding something. More likely it was just her personality: she was waiting for questions, eager to co-operate but patient and proper. Perhaps the need that Jack and Georgia had had to blurt out their stories was more suspicious.

Hal was asking her about Georgia and Carl.

"Well, um, they're nice, really," she said. "Um, I don't know what to say. They're... popular. They do argue a lot, with each other I mean. Georgia's very... upfront. Fiery. She says what she thinks. And she's quite... physical."

"Can you elaborate on that?" asked Hal.

"Well, um, she's sort of, sporty, and... I don't know, really. She... she and Carl have big rows sometimes, and... I've never actually *seen* them physically fight, but... well, I don't like to say."

Hal nodded. "Can you tell me in your own words what happened today, at the barbecue?"

"Well. We were in the garden. It was very hot. Georgia has this patio set, and fairy lights and everything, and they have a proper brick barbecue and a chiminea - is that what you call it? - and they even have a patio heater, although it was hot today, so it wasn't on. And we had a lot to drink. A *lot* to drink. We were talking, about all sorts of things. And Georgia and Carl argued a bit... I don't know, there was, like, a tension between them. And then, I remember..." She frowned, as if she was thinking very hard. There was something of a pantomime about Annette's gestures, and Rose wondered again whether this was a sign that she was lying, or just her normal manner. "Georgia went into the house. I think she got cross with Carl over something, but I can't remember what. She sort of stomped into the house. And then Carl went in after her. The back door goes into the kitchen... they both went into the kitchen... then, I don't know exactly, because Jack and I were talking... then, we heard a noise, something, in the kitchen, so we went to see. And there was, there was, well... Carl had been stabbed. There was blood everywhere. So Georgia must have stabbed him. I mean, I didn't see it, but she went in, and then he went in, and then he was stabbed."

"When you say you heard a noise," said Hal, "from the kitchen, so you went in - what was the noise?"

"Um, I don't know," Annette said. "A... noise. Something that made us go and look..." She took a deep breath, twisting her wedding ring. "It was awful." She shook her head. "The knife was... it was, it was stuck in his neck. There was blood just... We used, um, tea towels to try to put round his neck, to sort of stop the bleeding..." She put her hand to her mouth.

"Where exactly was Georgia when you came into the kitchen? What was she doing?"

"I don't know... She was screaming, or crying, I remember that. She wasn't holding the knife, it was in Carl's neck. She was standing up... yes, she was standing, sort of standing over him."

"Did she say anything?"

"She... I don't know. I think she said sorry at one point."

"Sorry?"

"Yes... I don't think she really wanted to kill him or anything. I think she just lost her temper and just grabbed the knife. The knife was out on the, the chopping board, for cutting lemons. She probably just grabbed it, and..." Annette started to gesture, and then stopped herself, and put her pale hands carefully on the table. She started twisting her ring again. "Isn't it awful? Poor Carl. How is he? Will he... I mean..."

"He's in a critical condition," said Hal.

"Awful," repeated Annette. "Has he... has he been able to say anything?"

Hal paused. "He hasn't made a statement yet."

Annette nodded. "I don't suppose he really knows what happened," she said. "I mean with the shock and everything. And it happened so quick, and we were all there. He's probably quite confused."

Hal looked at her but didn't say anything.

"Poor Carl," she added.

Hal looked thoughtful. "So," he said, "from what you've told us, the fingerprints on the knife will be Georgia's?"

Annette paused. "Yes. Although… to be honest, I think we all touched the knife. When he was bleeding, and we were using the tea towels to try to… we would all have touched the knife. We were trying to help him. So my fingerprints and Jack's fingerprints are probably on there too. In fact…" She looked as if she was thinking hard, her brow creased and her eyes narrowed. "In fact, I think I touched the knife earlier. Jack, too… I think we all sliced lemons at some point."

"I thought Georgia was making the drinks," said Hal.

"Well, yes, but we were all in and out of the kitchen, helping, chatting. I can't really remember but I think we probably all used the knife at some point."

"Jack didn't say that."

"Well, maybe he didn't." Annette shrugged. "What did Jack say?"

"He said you and he were in the garden the whole time."

"Well, we were mostly, but everyone was in and out, you know?"

"Alright," said Hal. He turned to Rose. "Was there anything else?"

Rose leaned forward. "Annette," she said, gently, "I just want to ask you a little bit about your relationship with Jack. We have evidence that the two of you are a bit, well, volatile, that you argue from time to time. Is that the case?"

Annette looked at her. "Um, no more than any other couple."

Rose was keeping her tone friendly and conversational. "We've heard you've got a bit of a temper."

Annette looked guarded. "Well, I wouldn't say that, not especially, no. We argue a bit, like any other couple."

Rose nodded. "Okay. We don't have any other questions at the moment."

Annette started twisting her ring again. "Will I… will I have to say all this in court? I mean, against Georgia? Will she have to go to court for this?"

Rose hesitated, wondering what Annette was afraid of.

"It's early yet," she said carefully, "but it is likely that one way or another all this will end up in court, yes."

"Oh, um… I don't really want to give evidence against Georgia. I mean, I didn't actually see her do it. I couldn't stand up in court against her."

"If this case goes to court," Rose said, "you'll only be expected to say what you saw, no more."

"But…" Annette looked anxious. "Um, I don't want to say anything in court, really."

Rose watched her. Annette's eyes were fearful but impenetrable, and Rose had no way of knowing what the fears were. "It's early days," she said. "We haven't finished investigating yet." She paused. "Is there anything you want to ask us?"

"Um…" Annette took a deep breath, but then shook her head. "No."

"Okay," said Rose. "We'll end this interview there. We will need to question you some more a bit later."

"Will you?" Annette looked up apprehensively.

"Yes." Rose paused, but Annette said nothing more. She looked down at her hands and retreated into her thoughts.

12

As Katrina took Annette back to her cell, Rose loitered in the custody area.

"You've come for another biscuit?"

Rose laughed. "No thanks." She was checking her phone. "Is that what you do all night down here? Eat biscuits?"

"We have soup, too," Nick told her, raising his plastic cup as evidence.

"Mmm… the soup from the machine, lovely."

"I know. You get served real food upstairs in CID, don't you? Silver service, I heard."

"That's right." She smiled and slipped her phone away.

"So what did the third suspect say?"

"She's blaming the wife."

"Not aliens."

"Thankfully not aliens."

"Did she see her do it?"

Rose sighed. "No. And she's… oh, I don't know, there's something odd about her. I don't really believe her. But then we can't believe any of them, can we? You can't tell who's lying so you have to assume they all are."

Nick shook his head. " 'There's no art to find the mind's construction in the face.' "

Rose raised her eyebrows.

Nick laughed. "*Macbeth*," he said. "We all quote Shakespeare down here in custody, didn't you know that? We're very cultured."

The back door buzzed. Nick eyed the monitor and pressed the release button. "Looks like we've got a crowd."

Rose stepped back from the desk and headed for the door. "I'll leave you to it."

There was a commotion coming in through the back door. Nick put his cup of soup on a lower shelf and cleared away pens and paperwork - literally clearing the decks, he thought to himself. Ready for the next onslaught. A uniformed officer appeared in the doorway. "Can we come through, Serge?"

"Come on in. What have you got?"

The officer left the commotion in the corridor and came up to put his elbows on the high desk. "We've picked up four lads in a stolen car. Driving like nutters down Broad Street. All of them with previous. One of them's seventeen, but the others are sixteen and fifteen, so we'll need to call parents in…"

"…or social services…"

"…and I think we should breathalyse the driver." The officer scratched his head wearily. "Only, we're not a hundred per cent who the driver was. We reckon they swapped seats as we approached them."

Nick nodded. "At this stage, breathalyse anyone you think might have been driving."

"That's what we thought."

Out in the corridor, the lads were testing the acoustics with whistles and high spirits. "Start bringing them through, one by one, so I can book them in," said Nick.

He noticed Aaron hovering at the end of the desk, trying to make eye contact. "Yes?"

"Jack McAllister says he's hungry."

Nick nodded. "Microwave him something." There was a stack of ready meals available. Aaron slipped round behind Nick into the kitchen as the uniformed officer led in a teenager in a baseball cap. Katrina appeared in the doorway.

"Can I have a word with you when you've got a moment, Serge?" she asked.

"Can it wait?"

"Yes." She disappeared.

Nick started tapping at the computer keyboard. "Name?" he asked the teenager.

"Alfie Lewis."

"Date of birth?"

"Um, Serge?" It was Aaron, behind him. Nick looked round. "Shall I give him spaghetti bolognese or cottage pie?"

"Ask him. Date of birth?"

Down in the cells, Georgia Lane had begun to shout again, and this time she was answered by the mocking catcalls of three teenaged boys.

13

Butland and Ehlen were back in the office. Jesse Butland was sitting on a desk, flipping a pen up in the air and catching it with one hand, while Tomas Ehlen sat very low in a seat, blowing on hot coffee.

"Go on, then," said Rose, pulling up a chair and sitting down.

"Are you ready for this?" Butland stopped throwing the pen, but he spun it around his knuckles while he talked. He was a fidgeter. "We've got statements from two of the neighbours. Both say Carl and Georgia Lane have big arguments, screaming matches, but no direct evidence of violence. But get this - one neighbour is convinced Carl Lane and Annette McAllister are having an affair."

"Go on."

"Apparently this Lane chap works at home - he's got his own business - and Mrs McAllister works shifts at a supermarket, so she's often at home in the day. And allegedly she pops round all the time, while Mrs Lane is at work. This is according to the woman at number eight - what was her name?"

"Lesley Baker," said Ehlen.

"Lesley Baker. She's a housewife, at home with little kids, peeping out round her curtains all day, apparently."

"So this is just… she's just seen Annette McAllister going in there?"

"Yes. Many times. I know, it's gossip, but…"

"But it's worth putting to Annette. And to Georgia too. In fact, it's worth putting to all of them. It might stir up something." Rose tapped her fingers on the desk. Did this mean anything? It could be silly gossip. It could be the basis of a motive. But there could be anything going on between these suburban couples - they could be swingers, they could all be having affairs, they could all be cocaine addicts, devil worshippers, obsessive stamp collectors - would any of it prove anything? The question was who picked up that knife at that moment. They could all have had motives. Fingerprints on the knife handle would be a thousand times more useful.

Rose rubbed her eyes. The lights in the CID office drained her. The phone rang, and Ehlen reached across to answer it. "Did any of the neighbours actually witness anything useful today?" she asked Butland. "Or rather, yesterday?"

Butland shook his head. "We spoke briefly to everyone in the surrounding houses. No-one heard anything until the police and ambulance turned up."

Rose tapped the desk thoughtfully.

Tomas Ehlen put the phone down. "That was the hospital," he announced, without looking up. "Carl Lane is dead."

Act Two

The Murder Weapon

1

The witching hour was past and the night had reached its deepest point: the small hours, when daylight seemed at its most distant and the town was asleep. Those who roamed the streets, still awake, were the few who clung to the edges or lived in the shadows: the drunks, the thieves, the drug addicts - the night people - and Nick knew that many of them would wash up at either the hospital or the police station, the two islands of light in a town submerged in sleep. Since medieval times the night watchmen had kept their torches burning from sunset to sunrise, peering into the darkness to challenge those who crept around under cover of night; now, uniformed officers patrolled the town and brought their captives to Nick's desk, to be identified and interrogated.

'Stars, hide your fires,' Nick thought to himself, 'let not night see my black and deep desires.'

Not that there was anything Shakespearean about PC Connor Whealdon.

"Look, it's a good bike, this," he was saying. "Adjustable shocks, hydraulic discs… and it's as light as anything, look."

He had arrested two of the regulars, Alice and Jerome, on suspicion of going equipped to steal. He'd found them pushing the bicycle along a back street, Jerome carrying a black rucksack that made a clanking noise. Over their protests, PC Whealdon had searched the bag and was not surprised to find it full of tools.

"I reckon they've had this out of someone's shed," he went on. He had brought the bike into the custody area and was handling it covetously and showing it to Nick. "It's an expensive one."

"It's my bike," objected Jerome, limply. He didn't expect to be believed. He was a skinny young man in skinny jeans, wearing a cross-shaped earring that hung from one ear and bounced off his shoulder.

"If you just told me where you got it from," PC Whealdon said, rocking the bike to and fro, "we could save a lot of time."

"He told you, it's his bike," chipped in Alice. She was about nineteen, with a pale face and bitten nails, and wore her hair strained back in a tight, tense ponytail. She and Jerome were heroin addicts, stealing for their dealer, and they were regularly in custody, apologetic, ferrety, sorry for themselves. "He told you."

"You'll have to sit in a cell while I trail all around town making enquiries," continued PC Whealdon. "Why don't you just tell me where you took it from?"

"It's my bike," insisted Jerome.

"Yeah? Where did you buy it?"

"From a bloke."

"What bloke?"

"Just this bloke."

PC Whealdon laughed. "Come on, Jerome, you can be more inventive than that. You're not even trying."

Nick could see Katrina looking at him and he remembered that she had wanted a private word.

"Let's just get them booked in," he said.

"But *I* haven't done anything!" objected Alice.

"You're telling me you're not a lookout, Ali?" said PC Whealdon.

"I'd only just bumped into him!"

"Listen, I'm going to book you both in," said Nick. "There's clearly enough to hold you on suspicion of going equipped. You can do all this properly in an interview room."

"But I didn't do anything!" cried Alice.

The phone rang. Nick had started putting Jerome's details into the computer so Katrina reached around him to answer the phone. "It's Mrs Beardsley," she said.

"I'd better take that," Nick said, and Katrina handed him the phone. Alice was continuing her objections in the background, and PC Whealdon was playing with the bike. Nick held the phone to one ear and put his finger in the other. "Hello?" he said. "Is this Mrs Beardsley?"

"*Miss* Beardsley. I got a message to call you."

"Yes, Miss Beardsley. We've got your son here, Drew. We've been trying to get hold of you. He's been arrested in a stolen car with three other boys…"

"No - no." She started to talk loudly over the top of him. "I don't want to know - I've told him, I'm not having any more of this - he's out of control, I'm washing my hands of him."

"The thing is, Miss Beardsley, Drew's only fifteen so he has to have a parent here…"

"No, no, no bloody way - I'm washing my hands of him, it was bloody embarrassing last time, I said never again…"

"But the thing is…"

"I don't want to know."

"The thing…" The line had gone dead.

Alice was still arguing her case. "So I was just walking down to Donno's house, right, and I saw Jerome and so I said hi and I just walked with him for a bit…"

Nick turned to Katrina. "Could you do me a favour and ring social services? We'll need the duty social worker for Drew Beardsley." Katrina nodded and took the phone.

"Come on..." Alice was sounding desperate. "I haven't touched that bike, you can check it for fingerprints."

"It's my bike," repeated Jerome.

"Sure it is," said PC Whealdon.

Aaron was hovering in the background. Nick finished typing Jerome's time of arrest into the custody record and then looked up. "Aaron?"

Aaron spoke slowly, even in a crisis. "That Brian Dunn, in cell six."

"Yes?"

"He's gone and been sick all over his cell."

Nick nodded. "Call for the cleaner. Will he need fresh clothes?"

Aaron looked blank.

"Call for the cleaner, and then take him to wash if he needs to; if he's really out of it, let me know, we might need to call the doctor." Nick had a sudden fear of Brian Dunn lying unconscious and choking on the floor of his cell.

"Come on..." Alice was saying. She came close to the desk, looking up at Nick earnestly. "Sergeant, please, look, I was just walking along with Jerome, I wasn't doing anything. Please."

Nick held his hands up. "We'll just get you booked in, and then we can sort all this out."

"Please! I can't go back to Ripley, please..." She started to cry. Ripley Hall was the women's prison. "I can't do that again."

Nick had begun to put her name into the computer. "Why, are you on bail for something, Alice?" The screen hung empty for a moment and then confirmed that she was on bail for shoplifting. "Here we go," he said, "you're on court bail for theft, next hearing date sixteenth June."

"Please, Sergeant, come on…" They both knew that if she was charged with a new offence, committed on bail, he would keep her in custody for court in the morning, and the court would most likely refuse to bail her again, and remand her to Ripley Hall. "I haven't done anything…" Snot was bubbling from her nose as she wiped her eyes with her fingertips.

"We'll get you booked in, and then we can sort it out," Nick repeated. He realised Aaron was still standing there. "Have you called for a cleaner?"

"Uh…"

Katrina passed Nick the phone and he held it out for Aaron. "Call the cleaner and then go and check if Dunn's okay."

"I can't, I can't do Ripley again," wept Alice.

"Listen," said Nick, wearily. "Just let me get you booked in, and then we can sort everything out."

2

Someone had to tell Georgia Lane that her husband had died.

"We could get the custody sergeant to do it," suggested Butland.

They were still in the CID office, the whole team, pondering their next move. It was now a murder investigation. Hal was twisting his swivel seat gently from side to side and Rose was tapping her pen on the desk. "I'll tell her," she said.

"We need to arrest them all for murder now," said Hal.

"I'll do that," offered Butland. Rose suppressed a smile. She knew that Butland wanted the glory of making a murder arrest. There was a prestige that came with reciting such important words - *I'm arresting you on suspicion of murdering Carl Lane. You do not have to say anything...* - a hush in the room, a sense of seriousness and weight that stood out from all the everyday work of burglaries and robberies; and Rose knew that Butland was the kind of guy who would boast in the pub, years from now: "You've never arrested anyone for murder? Oh yeah, I have…" He would carry himself that bit taller for having made three murder arrests.

"I think the wife should be told he's dead, though, I mean, before I arrest her for murder," Butland added. He didn't want to deal with any emotional fallout. He started nervously bouncing his pen off his knee.

"You don't think we should surprise her with the murder arrest?" said Rose. "That way we'd get her reaction under caution."

Butland's pen was a blur, it was twitching so fast. "I don't think that's a good idea," he said, "I mean, for her. She might freak out completely."

Rose was just teasing him. "It's okay," she nodded. "I agree, it would be cruel to let her know he's died by arresting her for murder. I'll tell her the news before you do the arrest."

It was, Rose believed, the job of the senior officer to do the difficult work, not the glamorous. She had always had a strong sense of duty. As a child, she had been the eldest daughter, the responsible one, the deputy; she always felt she had to be sensible and dependable. Even now that role still rested upon her: since her divorce, her family had assumed she would be the one who would be there for their ageing mother. Her sister and brother were both married with kids, but Rose was a childless divorcee, as plain and reliable as a Victorian old maid. Everyone saw her life as a parabola - up, up, and then down, down. She had left home, been to university and had a career, but she would end up a grey stressed middle aged woman cooking microwave meals for herself and her mother.

Already her mother would ring her nearly every day. "I've got this lump," she would say. "Just like a pea, but flatter, on the side of my neck. You'll have to come over and feel it. I've been reading about sarcoidosis but I'm worried it's lymphoma." She would have already consulted a series of doctors, but she never accepted their opinions as conclusive; she liked to accumulate a portfolio of medical opinion. "They haven't got to the bottom of this cough," she'd say. "I think I need another chest x-ray. That radiographer was useless. It's an art you know, reading an x-ray; they miss thirty percent of abnormalities." She scoured the internet for articles about mesothelioma and emphysema.

It was perhaps ironic that Rose's brother was a doctor. Their mother knew better than to call him, though: he would happily call her a hypochondriac to her face, and get away with it, because his mother was in awe of him. He was the brainy one, although he had struggled through medical school, retaking so many exams that he always seemed to be revising, reciting the names of arteries under his breath and sitting up late surrounded by thick books that bristled with post-it notes. He was a gynaecologist now, married to another gynaecologist, with two kids, living far away in the north of Scotland and never coming home to visit. "Once I get away from here," he used to say, when they were teenagers, "I'm never coming back." He found their mother infuriating. During their teenage years she was obsessed with food additives and e-numbers, artificial sweeteners and colours and preservatives and pesticides sprayed on vegetables and herbicides sprayed on wheat; it seemed as if everything they ate was poisonous. She dragged her children around sour-smelling little shops to find stunted organic potatoes and grey organic flour, and banned them from eating anything their friends ate. From time to time she would discover that a food they had thought was innocent - a simple tuna sandwich or cheddar cheese - was actually packed with mercury or growth hormones or antibiotics, and she would eradicate it from her kitchen and worry about how much her children had unwittingly ingested. Rose's brother now delighted in extolling the virtues of GM foods and scornfully debunking organic farming and clean eating.

Her little sister wasn't brainy, but she was the artistically interesting one, playing violin and studying textiles at college; she had married an executive who did something in the city and now lived an idyllic life in Dorset with four children, baking and finger painting while her husband commuted to London and back in his BMW. Rose never saw her either.

Rose had become what her mother called a 'career woman'. On the surface it sounded like a compliment, but in its depths the phrase swirled with strong currents of implication: she would never have a successful marriage, would never have children, would never be whole. Her mother was confident that she could ring Rose at any time on any evening and she would be available. On a Saturday night she would talk at length about the taste of the tap water and get Rose to google links between aluminium sulphate and Alzheimer's. Rose felt she was still tethered to her mother, and would be forever: the eldest child, the dutiful daughter, the one who couldn't escape.

"I guess I'll get this over with," she said, standing up and straightening her jacket. "We should let Georgia know he's dead sooner rather than later."

"Do you want me to come with you?" offered Sophie.

"No, that's okay, thanks."

"You might get a useful reaction from her," said Butland. "If she seems pleased, it's a giveaway it was her…"

"Yeah," laughed Hal, "if she punches the air, we've got her."

"Of course, if she is guilty, she'll play up her distress," said Butland. "You might find her reaction is over the top."

"Without knowing her well, it would be difficult to say whether someone's reaction is over the top," said Sophie, thoughtfully. "Some people are very dramatic. Some people are naturally reserved."

Rose picked up her folder, holding it like a shield. "Chase up any forensics on the knife," she said. "It would be a miracle if it's useful, but you never know."

"Miracles do happen," said Hal.

"If Georgia's fingerprints are on the knife and the McAllisters' aren't, we've got the basis of a case against her," said Rose. She knew that her team were operating on the assumption that Georgia was the killer, and she couldn't blame them. Simple statistics and experience told them that if someone was murdered, the culprit was most likely their spouse or lover. Each case, though, was unique - each set of circumstances was different, and people could be strange and baffling - there could be relationships and intentions and motives here that CID knew nothing about. Rose just hoped that Georgia *was* the killer; if she wasn't, then tonight she was living a nightmare.

3

Down in custody, Nick still hadn't had a chance to speak to Katrina. He had sent her down to Georgia Lane's cell to let DI Olding in. Alice and Jerome had both asked to see the duty doctor; they were no doubt hoping he would prescribe them something. Nick decided to ask the doctor to look at Brian Dunn, too. Dunn's cell was being mopped out slowly by the taciturn cleaner, and Dunn was now wearing a paper suit, his clothes having been stuffed into a bin bag to go home with him when he was eventually released. Nick was now on the phone trying to get hold of the officers who had arrested the four boys in a stolen car, because the mother of two of the boys, Stan and Alfie Lewis, had turned up, and someone from the front desk had brought her down to custody and deposited her with Nick.

"I'm doing my best with them," she was saying. "I've got the school on to me every other week, I mean, they're big lads now, what am I supposed to do?"

She was wearing what looked like pyjamas, but Nick didn't like to comment. He was leaving a message for the officers to call him; they seemed to have gone missing. "Their father's not interested, and I've got younger kids - I've got a little girl that's only five - I had to get a neighbour come and babysit. It's not fair on her, is it? And I've got work in the morning - I start at six. I'm not going to get any sleep now, am I?"

The cells were filling up, and Nick was beginning to feel that things were getting out of control. He called through to the officer who had arrested the possession of cannabis in cell five. "Are you ready to charge him? We're getting full down here - I want to charge him and bail him out." Mrs Lewis didn't stop talking while Nick was on the phone. "It's that Drew," she was saying. "He's the one. I've had nothing but trouble since they started hanging around with him." Nick put the phone down and shouted his thanks to the cleaner, who was leaving. Then he called out to Aaron. "Have you locked up Brian Dunn's cell?"

Aaron looked at him. "I think so."

"Can you go and check, please?"

"They won't get locked up for this, will they?" Mrs Lewis was asking. "When we were at court last time they said they had to stay out of trouble for six months, and that was only about two months ago."

"I don't know," said Nick. Katrina had made him a cup of tea some time ago and he could tell just from cupping his hand around the mug that it had gone cold. "I can't say what the youth court will do." He saw DI Olding and Katrina in the doorway. "Would you mind sitting on the bench in the corridor for a while, Mrs Lewis?" As she moved reluctantly away from his desk he caught DI Olding's eye. "All done?"

Rose looked strained. "She didn't take it well."

"Biscuit?"

Rose smiled. "The cure for all ills." She put her phone to her ear. "Sophie? I've told her - you can tell Butland he can come down and do the arrests. She didn't say anything significant. She was just upset and angry with me."

Katrina had come up to the desk. "She wants some paracetamol," she said. "Georgia Lane. Is that okay?"

Nick nodded. "Take her two with a cup of water. I'll note it on the custody record." He turned back to Rose. "Do you think the doctor should have a look at Georgia Lane? I've got a doc coming in to see some of the other prisoners."

"It wouldn't do any harm," said Rose.

"Can I see my boys now?" Mrs Lewis had already lost patience with sitting in the corridor.

"Just a moment." Nick picked up the phone.

"What does TWOC mean?" Mrs Lewis was looking up at the whiteboard, where TWOC was written beside her sons' names.

"Taking a motor vehicle without consent," explained Nick, with the phone to his ear. As his call went through, Rose slipped away, giving him a little wave. He waved back at her. "Is that Kyle? I've got Mrs Lewis here, mother of Stan and Alfie. Are you coming in to interview them?"

There was a pause. "Uh… we don't have a statement from the owner of the car yet. It's the middle of the night."

"Is the vehicle registered to any of the boys?"

"Well, no."

"Then you've got enough to interview them. Get in here." Nick rang off. Katrina was back at the end of the desk, trying to make eye contact, but at that moment two CID officers came strolling in.

"Sergeant… good morning. I'm DS Butland, this is DC Ehlen. We need you to bring out some of your guests so we can arrest them on suspicion of murder." Butland started to spread his paperwork out on Nick's desk.

"You can do that in their cells," said Nick.

"Huh?"

"You don't need them brought out here, do you? You can effect an arrest in a cell."

"Well…"

"Aaron! Could you take these officers down to Jack McAllister's cell please?"

"Um…"

"And Mrs Lewis." Nick was taking control now. "Mrs Lewis, the officer in charge of your sons' case is on his way here to speak to you. I need you to take a seat in the corridor to wait for him. We're very busy in here, as you can see." Finally, he turned to Katrina.

"I'm sorry, I know you've been trying to speak to me for ages," he said. "What can I do for you?"

The room had temporarily cleared, but Katrina still moved closer to him, and used a low, confidential tone. As she spoke, she smoothed her hair back behind her ears. "I was wondering; I know it's a lot to ask, but can I pop home? It's just… I've been ringing Stuart but he's not answering. He's probably just asleep - the morphine sends him off - but it would put my mind at rest if I could pop home. I could be back in less than an hour; there's no traffic at this time of night. I haven't had a break yet."

"Yes. Absolutely. That's fine." Nick was nodding vigorously. "We can spare you for a bit; you go. Absolutely."

The weight of life and death on Katrina made Nick feel clumsy and insensitive; and also light and insubstantial, like a fluttering moth. Anything he said would sound foolish. Katrina had lived through things; she had seen things, felt things, knew things; she was watching her husband, the man she loved, slowly die. Nick just kept nodding. "That's fine."

"Do you want me to check on Annette McAllister before I go?"

"No, that's fine; I'll take the CID officers into her and do the check then. You just go. Take an hour; we can manage."

"Thanks."

Nick watched her on his CCTV monitor as she walked to the back door; he buzzed her out and she slipped off into the night. He had never met Stuart, but he thought about him now, alone in the small hours, a man near his end. Like most people, Nick had, at one time or another, wondered aloud in idle conversations what he would do if he had only a few weeks to live; like most people, he had imagined he would seize the day - travel, make love, swim in moonlight. But he saw now that in real life, nearness to death was not an opportunity to embrace life with renewed energy but quite the opposite: life seeped away gradually, in a steady decline. The dying was itself a process that occupied those final weeks. If you felt sick, tired, and in pain, there was no will to travel the world or dance until midnight. What did it mean, then, to seize the day? Was it enough to enjoy a cup of coffee, the face of a friend, or a joke on TV that let you momentarily forget yourself? How could you grasp those precious final weeks? And how could anyone know, who had not been there themselves?

Nick's grandmother had died in a hospice. To Nick, then a teenager, it had seemed natural: she was old, and he had somehow assumed that the old were resigned to death. He didn't see her fear, but now he was older he thought that she must have been afraid. How could she not have been? He knew, too, that one day that fear would come to him, as it did to everyone.

The death of Carl Lane had made Nick pause, too, when Rose Olding had turned up in custody to tell him and to break the news to Carl's wife. Even the death of a stranger could be shocking. For so many hours the man had been in hospital, still alive, and it had begun to seem impossible that he could die. He was surrounded by doctors and drugs and machines; just as in a thousand scenes in a thousand hospital dramas, it had seemed that he would be saved - how could he not? He was not old or sick but young and broken, so surely he could be fixed, put back together again, reassembled like a faulty engine or glued like a cracked vase. While he was in hospital, in a 'critical condition', it had seemed that he was in the shadows between life and death, as if the two states blended into one another; but now he had died, and it was a shock to realise that death was irreversible, and it was all over.

Dying, Nick thought, was like falling: you were alive while it was happening, but the fall could only end one way. Perhaps life itself was just one long fall.

4

"So, what do we make of this?"

The forensic report on the knife had come through, in preliminary email form, and the knife itself was lying on the desk between them, imprisoned in a clear plastic bag. There was blood on the knife - on the blade and on the handle - and even speckled on the inside of the bag, as if a sample of air from the violent encounter had been trapped in there as well. It made the knife appear to possess a sinister intent of its own, as if it had been forced into the bag to restrain it. It was a huge knife, a knife that could chop melons or carve pumpkins, with a blade longer than the thickness of a man's neck. They were all looking at it.

"It could have been better," said Hal.

"At least we've got something to confront them with," said Butland.

"The knife or the report?"

"Both."

Rose nodded. "It's worth a try, but I don't think we'll get any confessions just yet." It seemed to her that the ceiling in the CID office was getting lower, pressing down as the night pressed on. There was something unsettling about the middle of the night, she thought: it was as if time had stalled, and she would always remain right here, under artificial light, closed in behind the shiny metal blinds with all these desks and blank screens and silent phones. It was a suffocating feeling. "You're right, Hal, the report would have been more useful if it had found less."

The forensics team had found fingerprints on the handle of the knife from all three of the suspects. It was an embarrassment of riches. The victim's prints were there, too - the forensics team had proudly uncovered and identified prints of good evidential value from four different individuals. The medics had all worn gloves, the knife had been removed carefully from the victim's neck and immediately bagged, and the forensic staff had worked quickly and effectively; but in terms of proving anything in this particular case, it was all useless.

"It doesn't help us at all," said Rose. She tapped the desk thoughtfully. "Next question: the neighbour's statement. This possibility of an affair between Carl and Annette. What do we do with that?"

Before anyone could speak, the phone rang. DC Ehlen reached for it.

"CID?"

He listened intently.

"Yes, she's here." He held the phone out to Rose. "It's the boss."

Rose hesitated but took the phone. For a moment she wondered whether to carry the conversation to somewhere more private, but she would have had to walk right across the open plan office and into the corridor, and it would have appeared to her team that she was nervous, or had something to hide. "Hello?" she said.

"Rose - I hear this stabbing has turned into a murder." DCI Newlyn was in charge of CID and worked office hours, so right now he was at home, probably sitting up in bed, or maybe in his living room in his pyjamas; he didn't sound sleepy. He never sounded sleepy. He was an alert, sharp man in his fifties, with a sharp nose and a sharp chin and a wiry, fatless body that spent an hour in the gym every morning. Rose wondered who had told him about the murder.

"That's right," she said.

"How's it going?"

"We're working through it," she said, trying to inflate her voice with confidence. "We're getting there. We've got three suspects - they were all in the house when it happened, it has to be one of them - and we've just started interviews. We've just received initial forensics, actually, just now. Early days still."

"Hmm." There was a short, sharp pause. "Do you need me to come in?"

"No, not at all. It's pretty straightforward really."

"Are you sure?"

"Yes, we're doing fine, working through it."

"Do you think you'll get to charge within twenty-four hours?"

"Uh, should do, yes, we're getting there."

"Good."

"It's only been" - she was calculating furiously - " about nine, ten hours since arrest; we're not even twelve hours in yet."

"Okay. Just remember that time can flash by quicker than you realise."

"Oh, I know."

"Anyway, I'll be in at seven."

"Yes."

"See you then." He was gone. She pressed the button on the phone and handed it back to Ehlen.

"Who called him, then?" asked Hal. Rose could have kissed him for asking - if she had raised the question herself, she would have looked anxious or upset. For a moment no-one spoke, and then Butland said, casually: "I sent him a message, just to keep him up to date. I thought that was the procedure."

No-one said anything, or made eye contact. Butland was sprawled in his chair, leaning across a desk; he had a sheet of paper pinned down with one finger, and was swirling it slowly round and round with his other hand. He didn't look up. "Okay," said Rose. "Where were we? The neighbour's statement. Is it just bollocks, or can we use it?"

"Again, I think we may as well confront them all with it," Hal said.

"I agree," nodded Rose. "The problem is, it gives all of them a motive. If Carl and Annette were having an affair, then Georgia could be jealous, Jack could be jealous, and even Annette could have a motive… spurned lover perhaps. This gives us something to throw at them all, but it doesn't give us anything to pin anyone down."

"Like the fingerprints," said Hal.

"Like the fingerprints. And then we come to Annette's 'new information'." She looked across at Butland.

He sat up in his chair and snatched up his sheet of paper with a flourish. "That's right," he said. "Comments following arrest for murder. Jack McAllister didn't say anything. Georgia Lane said 'You must be kidding.' But Annette McAllister said" - he read from his notes - " 'I've thought of something. It might be important.' So I told her we'd be down soon to ask her about it."

Rose nodded. "Interesting."

"Sadly it doesn't sound like she's about to confess," said Hal.

Rose tapped the desk, thinking.

"What I don't understand," said Sophie, "is why the McAllisters aren't desperate to point the finger at Georgia. I mean, if Georgia did it, they must know, so you'd think they'd screaming and pointing at her from the moment the bobbies arrived. And if *they* did it, you'd think they'd be blaming her just as insistently… but they both seem quite vague, kind of reluctant to say it was her. In fact, Jack was all set to throw out this idea of it being an accident."

"Maybe all three of them are in it together," Hal grinned. "Like an Agatha Christie plot."

"God, I hope not," said Rose. "Although we might end up having to consider the possibility."

"We could charge all three of them and dump it on the CPS," said Butland.

"Let's hope it doesn't come to that," said Rose. "Right, let's interview Annette again and see what she's got to say. Then we put it to her that she was having an affair with Carl, and that her fingerprints are on the knife. We won't tell her everyone else's prints are on it too."

"We'll go in mean this time," said Hal. He stood up and stretched.

"Perhaps we should have a second interview team?" suggested Butland. "Ehlen and I could question Jack McAllister."

"No," said Rose. "Consistency is better. Hal and I will do all the interviews. Let's have a bit of background research - you three can get busy googling all our suspects: look at Facebook, Twitter, find their accounts… and find out about Carl's business. Just see if anything comes up."

Butland looked unenthusiastic.

Hal picked up the knife by a corner of the plastic bag. "Let's go," he said.

The CID office opened out onto a corridor painted the colour of milky tea; at the end were double doors into a stairwell, a self-contained vertical shaft where the sound of footsteps echoed off the hard surfaces. On the lower landing there was a window without curtains or blinds, but all that could be seen was a streetlight, so bright and near that it crowded out any view. The world beyond was a black void. It sometimes felt to Rose, when she worked nights, as if the police station was an island, or even a ship, alone in a vast empty sea. She remembered, too, a story she had read as a very young child, about a whole town put to sleep by a sorcerer so that dawn never came; and she was sure that that story had planted in her mind a tiny irrational fear that her night shift might never end. The small hours were so slow and eccentric, as if time had been corrupted.

Rose and Hal continued down the stairwell to the very bottom, where a security door could let them into the custody suite. Hal punched in the code and the door unlocked with a half-hearted beep. The custody suite was busy. Nick was behind the desk looking hot and stressed, and two uniformed officers were taking a youth and his mother into an interview room. A grumpy-looking man in a v-neck jumper and check shirt was leaning on the custody desk frowning at a laptop in a battered case. Rose stepped up to the desk beside him.

"Busy night?" she smiled at Nick.

"You could call it that. Are you hoping for an interview room?"

"You're that busy?"

"I'm sure we can accommodate you." Nick grinned. "I was just about to ask the doc to see Georgia Lane."

The grumpy man looked up. "You've got another one for me?"

Nick nodded. "Just one more."

"That's okay," said Rose. "We want Annette McAllister first."

"I'll get her out for you."

Nick came out from behind his desk with a bunch of keys, hitching up his trousers and smoothing down his shirt. There was a solidity about him, Rose noticed, a dependable good humour, a quality that made her feel warm and calm. He moved comfortably through space. When he returned from the cells with Annette he wasn't holding her arm but rather walking beside her companionably and sympathetically. He directed them all to an empty interview room and looked at his watch, so he could note the time on the custody record.

"We will want to interview the other two again," said Rose. "Could you call their solicitors for us?"

Nick smiled at her. "No problem." He held the door of the interview room open for them. "Enjoy."

Hal took Annette through the preliminaries, confirming her details for the camera, and then Rose took over.

"Just to clarify, Annette: a short while ago a detective came to tell you that Carl has now sadly died, and that you're under arrest for murder - you remember that?"

Annette was sitting with her pale, turquoise-tipped hands folded in front of her demurely, and she turned her face up towards them wearing a sorrowful expression. Everything she did and said seemed to be carefully delivered - but Rose had no way of knowing whether that was a sign of falsity. "Yes," she said. "It was awful news. Poor Carl."

"Yes. Now, when the detective spoke to you, you said you had remembered something, some new information?"

"That's right." Annette sat up eagerly, like a child who knew the answer to a teacher's question. "I've thought of something."

"What's that?"

"Well." Annette re-arranged her hands. "The thing is, thinking about it now, I think there was an intruder."

"An intruder."

"Yes. You know I was saying there was a sort of noise, from the kitchen, but I couldn't remember what? Well, I've been thinking about it and I think there was someone in the house." She started twisting her wedding ring. "I think there was some sort of noise, in the house, and that was why Carl went in."

"What sort of noise?"

Annette chewed her lip as if she was thinking intently. "I can't say. It didn't seem important at the time, but now I'm thinking it might have been a burglar that killed Carl."

"A burglar."

"Yes. Carl has a lot of valuable records, you know - it's his business, selling rare vinyl, and there are records in their back bedroom worth hundreds of pounds. Maybe thousands."

"You think there was a burglar."

"Yes. Well, I don't know, I'm just saying there might have been a burglar. All the downstairs windows were open because it was so hot; anyone could have got in easily."

"But this was daytime on a Sunday - weren't there lots of people around? Children playing?"

"Yes, but burglars can be very sneaky. Lots of people knew about Carl's business. There was a whole piece on him in the paper - he's a local businessman. He might even have cash in the house."

"Annette." Rose had pulled out her handwritten notes. "In your last interview you said - here it is - you said that Georgia went into the house first, into the kitchen, after she and Carl had had an argument. And then you said Carl went in after her. And then you said some sort of noise made you and Jack go in, and you found them both in the kitchen, and Carl had been stabbed. So if there had been an intruder, Georgia would have seen him, wouldn't she?"

"I don't know. Maybe she went into another room. Maybe she went in and went to the toilet or something, and then Carl went in to the kitchen, and the intruder came down the stairs and they saw each other and the intruder stabbed him and then ran into the front room and got out the window."

"Without Georgia seeing or hearing anything?"

"Yes."

"Your fingerprints were on the knife, Annette." Rose nodded to Hal and he brought out the knife, in its bloody bag, and laid it down on the table. Annette looked at it.

"Oh, poor Carl," she said.

"Your fingerprints are on the knife," Rose said, "not an intruder's."

Annette was staring at the knife. "Like I said, I touched the knife when I was trying to help Carl. And I think I cut some lemons too."

There was a pause.

"We have something else," said Rose.

Annette laced her fingers and looked up.

"We have evidence that you and Carl were having an affair."

Annette looked at her. Rose looked back. Annette's lips parted slightly in surprise, and for a moment or two she said nothing. Her hands didn't move. Then she said: "Well, we were good friends, but we weren't having an affair. I mean, Carl and I, we got on well, but I would never be unfaithful to Jack." She put her hands up to her face, and sniffed. "Poor Carl... this is so awful." Suddenly her eyes widened and she looked at Rose. "Maybe that's why she did it."

"What?"

"Maybe that's why Georgia killed Carl. Because she thought he was having an affair with me. Maybe that's why she was so angry with him."

"But you just said an intruder killed him."

"That's just a theory. It's more likely to be Georgia, isn't it?"

Rose could sense Hal, next to her, smothering a snort of frustrated laughter. "Look, Annette," she said, leaning forward. "We don't want you to come up with theories about what happened. This isn't a detective story. This is real life, and a man is really dead. We want you to tell us what happened. You were there. You know what happened. All this nonsense about intruders is telling me you've got something to hide. What are you hiding, Annette?"

Annette looked at her intently. "I'm just trying to help," she said. She sounded prim. "I told you exactly what happened. We were drinking in the garden, Carl and Georgia weren't getting on. Georgia went in, then Carl went in. Then Jack and I went in, and Carl had been stabbed." She stared at the knife. "It looks bad for Georgia, doesn't it?"

5

After the interview, Rose and Hal tried to find a corner of the custody suite to huddle in. There was an argument going on at the desk. A woman in a onesie was red-faced and shouting at Nick. "They're not pinning this on my boys!" She was furious. "It was that Drew! He was the one what was driving!" Nick was trying to calm the woman down, while two uniformed officers backed away. Rose and Hal moved into the corridor. The grumpy doctor was perched on the bench, typing into his laptop, and he glanced up just long enough to scowl at them.

"So… can we just ignore this intruder nonsense?" wondered Rose.

"It's obviously rubbish," said Hal.

"But we have to cover ourselves," said Rose. "Shit, I should have asked her more about the layout of the house and the windows, and what they could see from the garden. I could do with visiting the scene myself." The woman in the onesie was still shouting at Nick. Rose leaned against the cool bleach-scented wall. "Right. You call forensics and tell them we need to consider the possibility of an intruder. Any strange DNA or prints. Shit, this is a mess. I'm calling Butland."

She moved further down the corridor and she and Hal both made calls, in spite of the shouting in the background. One of the uniformed officers was now repeating "Hey, hey hey," at the woman, ineffectually. In the cells someone was singing.

Rose called Butland.

"Annette's great new information is that she thinks there might have been a burglar. She says there were windows open downstairs. I need you to pin down exactly who went in and out of there - all the bobbies, all the medics - in case we have to eliminate DNA, and I want you to get on to all the officers who attended the scene - wake them up if you have to - and ask them if the downstairs windows were open, and if any of the suspects mentioned the possibility of an intruder being around."

"She says there was a burglar?"

"Yes, it's a wild goose chase, I know, but we have to cover ourselves. In fact, it wouldn't hurt to tee up some uniformed officers to go round the whole street in the morning and ask all the neighbours if they saw anything suspicious - any strangers, heard any arguments, know anything at all - not just the neighbours you spoke to, but everyone far and wide. It's a murder investigation, we can commandeer some bobbies to do house to house."

"Right you are."

"It's a mess, this one."

"Do you think we should call in the boss?"

"No! God, this is all just rubbish, a sideshow." Rose took a breath. "We're going into the second interview with Georgia now. That should be more fruitful."

She ended the call and looked up at Hal. He was grinning at her last comment. "That's optimistic," he said.

Rose was straightening her clothes and looking determined. "Right," she said. "We need to be clever about this. We need to get tough on Georgia. Show her the knife. Tell her about the affair. She might not confess but she might make a mistake, say something that implicates herself… I'm going to get her to go over what happened again, to see if she's consistent. And I'm not going to tell her about this intruder thing. The last thing we want is to give her a way out."

Hal nodded.

"Are we ready?" Rose asked.

"We're ready."

6

"We went to B&Q," said Georgia, suddenly.

The interview had begun calmly. Georgia had been given some sort of mild sedative by the doctor, and she had become quieter, even withdrawn... sad, Rose thought, sad was the right word. Sad, and dignified. She reminded Rose of a tiger in captivity. She had repeated her account of events - she had been upstairs, fixed her makeup, taken her time; there were no raised voices downstairs, nothing to make her think something was wrong, nothing to prepare her for walking into her kitchen and finding her husband on the floor with a kitchen knife in his neck.

"Your fingerprints are on the knife," said Rose.

"Of course they are. It's my knife."

"The thing is, Georgia," said Rose, "you're trying to make us believe that the McAllisters, these neighbours of yours who you only meet up with for the odd barbecue, had some kind of motive to actually murder your husband. Why would they do that?"

Georgia stared at her. "I don't know," she said at last. "Ask them."

"It just seems to me," Rose went on, "far more likely that you, his wife, would have a reason to lose your temper. We're not saying you planned this, Georgia, this obviously wasn't planned. This was a spur of the moment thing. All marriages have tensions, don't they? It's easy to flip and do something you regret in the heat of the moment. We've all been there. You'd had a few drinks, it was a hot day, maybe you didn't really know what you were doing, you just grabbed the knife... just tell us what happened, Georgia. Let's get this over with."

Georgia was looking at her intently. When Rose stopped speaking, she leaned in and said, quietly but very clearly: "I did NOT stab him. There was no argument. I love him. I loved him. Shit." She took a breath, and looked at the table.

Rose paused. She had intended at this point to put to Georgia that Carl and Annette were having an affair, but it seemed such a cruel thing to say. It sometimes felt to Rose as if these interviews were pantomimes, and the suspects were mere actors, performing just another 'case'; but when she stopped to think, it alarmed her that these were real people, with real tragic lives. When she questioned a man who had tried to strangle his girlfriend there had been a real, terrifying struggle between them and before that months of love and hate; when she questioned a woman who had pushed her elderly mother down the stairs there had been a lifetime of difficult feelings and abusive love on both sides. It was all real, all complicated, all human.

"It's just a job," her ex-husband, Gavin, had said to her once. "You can't get emotionally involved in people's lives, you'd go mad. You wouldn't be able to do your job. You're there to find out what happened and put the facts before a court."

Rose had never thought of herself as someone who got emotionally involved. She had always been calm and intellectual about her work, and she thought Gavin was being patronising. "I know that," she told him, "I'm just saying, sometimes it hits you that these are people, not just crimes to be solved... I suppose what I'm saying is, it's all just so sad. When you charge someone, it's not a victory."

Gavin laughed. "Perhaps you should have been a social worker," he said.

Now, Rose paused, wondering how to put the affair to Georgia. Hal always said it was safest to assume everyone was guilty. "Innocent until proven guilty is the jury's job," he said. He was right. It was likely that Georgia was guilty, and Rose's job was to catch her out. To get a confession. Gavin was right, too: if she worried about a suspect's feelings, she wouldn't be able to do her job properly.

It was as Rose was hesitating that Georgia volunteered, suddenly:

"We went to B&Q."

Everyone looked at her.

"That morning," she said. "Yesterday, whatever it is now. Sunday morning. We went to B&Q to get some of that gel for lighting barbecues, and some citronella candles."

She looked down at her hands, at the chunky rings and her perfect nails, and the roughly bunched elastic cuffs of the paper suit.

"It was going to be a hot day, you could already tell. We drove down to B&Q, and they had all the summer stuff out, all the patio sets and garden swings, and they had these inflatable hot tubs, like paddling pools for grownups - we were looking at these inflatable hot tubs and thinking it might be a laugh to get one. Carl was really into the idea. And we were talking about our holiday - we've booked to go to Portugal next month, just for a week; it's a beautiful hotel with one of those pools overlooking the sea, an infinity pool. And when we were driving back from B&Q we passed the Balti House and I said it's been ages since we had a takeaway and Carl said let's get one on Wednesday."

She stopped.

"And now, this…"

She stopped and shook her head. "And you think I did this. Why, why would I do this?"

There was a pause.

Rose broke the silence. "We have evidence," she said, evenly, "that your husband was having an affair with Annette McAllister."

Georgia's solicitor spoke up. "What kind of evidence?"

"A statement from a neighbour."

Georgia released a sarcastic laugh, like a snarl. "That's ridiculous. Fuck, are you serious?"

"You and Carl maybe argued about this…"

"You're mad!" Georgia was shaking her head. "You're ridiculous. This is just silly… gossip, some idiot neighbour, some jealous… of course Carl wasn't having an affair. Carl and Annette?" She laughed. "Annette? Have you met Annette? She's as dull as dishwater, she's a little mousey thing, Carl wouldn't… you're mad.

"Me and Carl, we were…" She was groping for strong enough words. "We were *real*. You know what I mean? We were in love, we were living life, we were going somewhere… Jack and Annette are like sad little half-people, living a dull little life doing dull little jobs waiting for dull little kids to come along… they were jealous of us. Jealous of our spark, our passion. Our realness. That's why they wanted to destroy Carl. They were jealous."

There was silence, as Georgia stopped to wipe away a single tear and then looked fiercely across the table.

Rose could feel this case slipping away from her. It was nearly two o'clock in the morning. The night seemed to be taking her in circles: the interviews were getting nowhere, the suspects were going around and around and there was no physical evidence to prove anything.

"Are you trying to tell me," she said, doggedly, "that you and Carl never argued? Never raised your voices?"

"Of course we argued," said Georgia. "But we never hit each other, never hurt each other. And yesterday we didn't argue, not once. Stop trying to say I did it…" She was crying properly now. "This is awful. I've lost… How can you keep saying this?"

"Do you have any more actual questions for my client?" asked the solicitor.

"No." Rose felt defeated. "We'll stop there for now."

She looked up at the clock and wondered what to do next.

7

There was something faintly disgusting about a half-eaten sandwich, even when he had half eaten it himself. Nick had brought a ham and mayo from home in a small discoloured tupperware box, but he had been distracted by work after just a few mouthfuls, and now it looked like the remains of a dead sandwich, rubbish rather than food. It was squashed and misshapen, spilling ragged ham and greasily extruded mayonnaise that was already becoming curdled and translucent. He snapped the lid back on the tupperware.

"Okay," he said to the disgruntled young officer on the other side of the desk. "Where are we with this, Kyle?"

Kyle pulled a face. "Well, we can charge all four of them with the TWOC, but the car was doing about fifty down the middle of the road, so I'd like to charge dangerous driving too." He leaned an elbow on the desk and swivelled around to his partner. "Ash and me are pretty sure it was the one in the cap that was driving, but by the time they got the doors open it was the one in the grey hoodie what was sat in the driver's seat."

"And the one with the cap is?"

"Alfie Lewis."

"And the grey hoodie?"

"Drew Beardsley."

"And in interview?"

"Oh, they're all doing this." Kyle pointed his fingers in opposite directions. "No-one was driving. And it was all someone else's idea."

"Can we charge them all with dangerous driving?" asked Ash. "Joint enterprise, like?"

Nick sighed. "Not really. Did you see them change places?"

"Oh, they was all bobbing about in the car," said Kyle.

"I thought the other kid was in the front at one point," chipped in Ash. "You know, the older kid, the seventeen year old. He's wearing that red t-shirt, he stands out."

"Shit, don't give us another curveball," said Kyle. "I'm confused enough as it is."

"What did he say in interview?" asked Nick.

"Not much," said Kyle. "He's a bit simple."

"He said he was in the back, like, the whole time," said Ash. "He said he didn't know who was driving."

Nick hesitated. "When you say he's a bit simple…"

"Yeah, he's pretty slow."

"…do you mean he has learning difficulties? You interviewed him without an appropriate adult, didn't you?"

Kyle and Ash looked at Nick.

Nick sighed. "We might need a social worker for him."

"Oh come on, Serge," said Kyle, "I didn't mean, you know… he's just a bit on the slow side."

"Have you checked his record? Does he usually have an appropriate adult with him for interview when he's here?"

Kyle said nothing.

"He's not been in care, has he?"

"I don't know, Serge, do we really have to…"

"Check his record, check whether social services are involved with him, check whether he had an appropriate adult with him when he was last under arrest. Then" - Nick took a breath - "then, both of you write statements about exactly what you saw, statements you'd be prepared to swear to in court, and then we'll decide who to charge with driving. It'll probably be Alfie *and* Drew, but I want your signed statements first."

Kyle exchanged a look with Ash, and they sulkily moved away from the desk, just as Rose and Hal came in from the corridor. "Finished your interview?" Nick asked.

Rose nodded wearily.

"Aaron!" Nick called. "Can you put Georgia Lane back in her cell?"

Rose came up to the desk, but at that moment the phone rang, and Nick picked it up. "Custody."

"I've got good news, Serge - I've solved the bicycle mystery." It was PC Whealdon. "We have one very impressed member of the public. The bike was registered - there was a number etched on the frame - and I got the owner's name and address and woke him up to inform him we'd recovered his bike, even before he knew it was stolen."

"Impressive."

"I took it round to him - chap in his pyjamas, very surprised. He's identified it. It was in a shed - I was right - they'd taken the padlock right off, unscrewed the bracket and removed the whole thing. He's going to look through the shed in the morning to see if anything else is missing."

Rose was waiting at the desk. She looked down at her phone, scrolling through a message. She looked tired and worried. Still listening to PC Whealdon, Nick reached under the desk and put a packet of biscuits in front of Rose. She looked up and a grin broke across her face.

"I got a quick statement, though, so I can charge the bicycle theft," PC Whealdon was saying. "Burglary of a shed."

"That's great," said Nick. "So are you coming back now to interview Alice and Jerome?"

"Will do." He rang off. Rose hadn't taken a biscuit, but she was looking humorously at Nick.

"We need Jack McAllister out now," she said.

"I shall fetch him myself." Nick swept past with the keys. Georgia Lane's solicitor was standing in the doorway, tucking away her phone. She looked up at Nick and Rose.

"Well," she said, "it won't be me for the next interview. The boss has decided to come in."

"Huh?"

"Mister Paley." She worked at Bryants solicitors, and Philip Paley was one of the senior partners. "Now it's a murder he wants to take over. He'll be coming down here in person."

"We *are* privileged," laughed Nick. "At least you'll be able to go home and get some sleep."

"Not much. I've got to email him a report of everything that's been said. And I've got appointments in the office from nine."

"I'll buzz you out," said Nick, "and then I'll get Jack." He stepped back around the desk, jangling keys, and reached to press the button. As he stood, holding it down, Aaron came out of the back kitchen. He was holding a small plastic tub of bright red pasta and stirring it with a thin plastic spoon, all the while peering into it intently as if something treacherous might be hiding in the sauce.

"Did you put Georgia Lane back in her cell?" Nick asked him.

Aaron looked up blankly.

Nick took his finger off the door release button and turned to Rose.

"Where's Georgia Lane?"

Rose just looked at him.

"Shit."

These moments of panic always seized Nick in the stomach. He experienced crisis as a physical, visceral clenching: everything was suddenly squeezed, from the organs inside his body to his field of vision - the world closed in and all sounds became louder, all lights brighter, all colours harsher. Memories flickered rapidly through his mind: that time when Joe was a toddler and fell off the top of the slide, that time when he went to pick Lucy up from infant school and couldn't see her, that time when a van crashed into the back of his car and he found himself suddenly facing the sky. It was as if there was a thread of crisis running through life, a deep core from birth to death, and every now and then the calm normality of the day-to-day would unexpectedly drop away and expose the core and things would go wrong; deeply, devastatingly wrong. He had to keep breathing against the clenched feeling, and keep calm, keep moving along the surface as if it was still there.

"Where's Georgia Lane?"

Hal was in the corridor, engrossed in his phone. He looked up, startled by Nick's voice. "I... I don't know, we left her in the interview room with her solicitor."

"She might still be there," said Rose. She had come up behind Nick. Her voice was steady. They moved together down the corridor. "We were in room three."

Nick flung open the door. Georgia Lane was sitting there, alone, with her white paper arms on the table and her head on her arms, and she looked up with a start when the door opened. Nick stopped, although it felt as if his insides continued to fly forwards. "There you are," he said, breathlessly.

Georgia Lane looked at him and her lip started to curl into a smirk. "Did you think you'd lost me?"

8

"I just want to go home now," said Jack McAllister.

He had been asleep in his cell, and now, under the bald lights of the interview room, he looked tired and confused, even tearful. His breath smelled bad and slowly permeated the small room. He rubbed his beard. "I just, you know, this is all so…" His eyes were pink. "Can I see Annette? Just to speak to her?"

"I'm afraid not," said Rose. "Not while the investigation is continuing."

While Jack had become more dishevelled, his solicitor, Sam Stead, had been home and showered and dressed in his Monday morning suit: he had leapt the gap between late night and early morning and he now looked like the first commuter of the day. His appearance made Rose feel that time was running out. The windowless room was as disorientating as a cinema: outside it could be pitch darkness or bright daylight. They were a strange collection of people in a strange nether-world.

"Is she okay?" Jack asked. "Annette?"

"She's fine," said Rose.

Jack rubbed both hands over his face.

"I want you to tell us again what happened at 6 Riverside View," Rose said.

"He's already told you," said Sam Stead.

"He was vague," said Rose. "And contradictory. I want him to go over it again, in more detail."

Jack was shaking his head. "I don't know," he said. "I don't know, it all happened so quickly. One minute we were in the garden, you know, having a great time, and then, honestly? I don't know what happened. Georgia and Carl were in the kitchen, and she stabbed him, she must have stabbed him. Me and Annette were in the garden. I can't believe he's dead. It's awful... he's actually dead. Poor Carl."

"Let me ask you some questions," said Rose, briskly. "Was anyone else there apart from you and Annette?"

"No."

"A burglar?"

"No."

"Did Carl and Georgia have an argument in the garden?"

"No. Not that I remember."

"Why did you and Annette go into the house? Did you hear a noise, a scuffle?"

Jack scratched his beard and thought. "I don't know," he said at last.

"What alerted you that something had happened? What made you and Annette go into the kitchen?"

"I don't know. It all happened so quickly. It was such a shock."

"Did Georgia go upstairs?"

"I don't know."

"Did she come downstairs?"

"No... no. She was in the kitchen."

"Who went into the house first, Georgia or Carl?"

"I don't know, to be honest. I wasn't paying attention, you know?"

"You said before that Georgia told you it was an accident."

"Yeah, but I don't think it was."

"When did she tell you that?"

"I don't know. Before we were arrested... I don't know, honestly. It was all confusing. I'm sorry."

Sam Stead had stopped making notes, and was fiddling with his silver-tipped pen. The white cuffs of his shirt were very sharp and clean, emerging crisply from the sleeves of his dark blue suit. He looked like he had somewhere else to be. Rose paused, tapping her own pen on the thick old polish of the long-suffering wooden table.

She felt that she was trudging through these interviews as if through mud: uninspired, her questions followed an obvious path, and discovered nothing but more mud. She felt tired and blunt. If only she could find the magic question, the key... a while ago, in a robbery case she had led, one of the suspects had blundered into boasting when she asked him if he had a second car, and the resulting forensics from his BMW had incriminated not just him but the whole gang. A magic question would be so useful here - or if not a magic question, she would at least be grateful for a web: in most cases, a successful interview was one where the questioning was slow and sticky, steadily wrapping the suspect up in circumstantial evidence - he accepted he was there, yes, perhaps at that time, yes, the witness had no reason to lie, that hat was his if his DNA was in it and yes, the description of the car could fit his - all the "yes, but..." answers were gradually closed down until the suspect was trapped, stuck to the facts, with nowhere to go.

But this case... there were no witnesses, no useful forensics, nothing Rose could confront anyone with. Nothing the suspects had to account for beyond the fact of a knife in a man's neck, a knife all three of them had touched in trying to save him. Rose was fumbling, she knew that. She looked across the table at Jack McAllister and she had nothing.

"I was thinking, you know," he said, "maybe there's life insurance. You know, Carl's got his own business and he's been making a lot of money - a *lot* of money - so maybe he took out life insurance, and if they haven't been getting on, well, if they got divorced Georgie wouldn't get anything, would she, because they don't have kids... so maybe she killed him to get the life insurance, you know? It's just a thought."

"You're saying Georgia planned this?"

"I don't know, it's just a thought."

"I'm not asking you to speculate."

"Sorry." He rubbed his face.

"Do you have any more questions?" asked Sam Stead. "We seem to be just treading the same ground."

"Georgia says Annette stabbed Carl," said Rose.

Jack looked blank for a moment, and then started shaking his head. "That's... well, no, that's not what happened. Really? She's trying to say it was Annette? No, no, we came into the kitchen together and he was already stabbed... that's mad, that is. Why would *Annette* stab Carl? *Annette*?"

"Georgia says Annette has a temper."

"That's rubbish."

"Georgia says you and Annette have big fights. She says she saw Annette physically attack you."

"What? No, of course not."

"This was an occasion around Valentine's Day when you had Georgia and Carl round for dinner. You argued and Annette said you didn't really want children, and flew at you."

"No! That never happened. Me and Annette... no, that never happened. We both want children, we've never argued about it. Annette would never attack me... you've seen Annette, she's tiny. Annette's quiet, gentle - you ask anyone. Now, Georgia, she's the one with the temper. She's, you know, passionate, full on, aggressive; I could definitely see her grabbing a knife."

"Have you ever seen Georgia hit anyone?"

"Well no, but people are different in private, aren't they? She might have attacked him loads of times for all I know. She's really big and strong, she's very physical, you know? She's a personal trainer, that's her job. And she's volatile - I reckon he said something to her in the kitchen and she just flipped. And now she's saying it was Annette... it's transference, isn't it? She's making out Annette lost her temper when it was herself, it was Georgia. She's messed up, you know? She must be to have done this."

"But you told us it was an accident."

"No, I just didn't want to believe it, that's why I said that, I wanted to believe it was an accident because it was so awful. You know, I mean, it's murder, isn't it? Murder."

"It is murder," agreed Rose. "That's why we need you to be clear, Jack, and honest."

"I'm telling you as best as I can remember."

Rose tapped the table. "We have something else we need to ask you about. We've been making further enquiries, and we have a new piece of evidence."

Jack looked at her expectantly, and she allowed a moment of silence before she said: "We have reason to believe Carl and Annette were having an affair."

Jack looked surprised, and then laughed. "That's ridiculous. Carl and Annette? I don't know who's told you that."

Rose said nothing.

"There's no way... I mean, Carl's like, a really cool guy, you know? Him and Annette - he wouldn't see Annette like that, you know? That's just rubbish. Who told you that?"

"We're not able to disclose that at this stage."

"Is this just local gossip?" asked Sam Stead.

"I can't disclose that at this stage," repeated Rose.

"Well, my client's answered your question," said Sam.

There was a pause.

"I just want to go home," Jack said. "Georgia stabbed him, it's obvious. Why don't you just let me and Annette go home?"

9

Katrina had returned, but Nick hadn't had a chance yet to speak to her. Her face, as ever, gave nothing away. Alice had begged for food and Katrina had set off down to her cell with a microwaved plastic lasagne and a plastic spoon. There was a moment of peace; Nick locked Jack McAllister back in his cell and then pulled out his cigarettes and lighter.

Rose was in the corridor, looking at her phone and pinching her lower lip.

"Not going well?" Nick offered.

Rose shook her head. "No breakthroughs," she said. "No smoking gun." She looked up at Nick, and he saw that her eyes were soft grey in the flat light of the corridor. She rubbed one of them with a delicate fingertip. "No confessions."

"You want us to twist some arms?" Nick grinned. "Do it the old fashioned way?"

Rose laughed. She saw the packet of cigarettes in his hand. "Do you think I could have one of those?"

"Of course. You clearly need something stronger than a biscuit."

He walked ahead of her to the back door, and Rose felt an unexpected flush of warmth, that feeling of liking a boy - a teenager's feeling - an awkward, happy, nervous, excited, embarrassed, giddy feeling; a silly thing, she thought, a crush. It seemed, tonight, that every time she encountered Nick Toft they ended up grinning at one another. She had met him before, had seen him around, but had never really spoken to him like this, never really *seen* him… what was it that made a person suddenly interesting, suddenly in focus? It was probably silly. He was just one of the custody sergeants, as steady and plain as the building itself.

They stepped outside. The night was still warm, with the perfect breeze, and the tall lights of the car park were bright and eager. Nick put his boot in the door so it wouldn't close. "It's okay," he explained, "I disable the buzzer when I come out, so it won't be shrieking in there." Through the crack of the door Rose could see the greasy light on the corridor wall, but outside it was cool and fresh. "Here you go."

He handed her a cigarette. She felt the crackle of tobacco through the thin paper, and put the tip between her lips, leaning close for him to light it. The flame danced a little in the breeze.

It had been a while since she last smoked, so the first draw went straight to her head: an elated, almost swooning sensation. "I did give up," she said, "about a year ago. Well, actually, I gave up years and years ago, when I was, gosh, early twenties; but then I started again when I got divorced. And then I stopped again. And then sort of started again."

"A serial quitter."

"That's right."

"For me, it's more of a double life. When my kids were born I gave up, but I just couldn't stop at work - and it's been like that ever since: I'm a smoker at work and a non-smoker at home."

"How old are your kids?"

"Sixteen and fourteen. My boy's just doing his GCSEs." He tapped ash on to the ground. "Do you have kids?"

"No." Rose tapped her ash too, and it fluttered in white flecks between them.

"I'm divorced too, of course," volunteered Nick. "Everyone is, on the force."

Rose grinned. "Everyone."

"Married to the job, they say."

"My husband was a copper, too," said Rose. "So I guess we were doubly doomed. We were both married to the job."

It was true, she thought - she and Gavin had both been ambitious; perhaps even in unacknowledged competition with each other. Gavin joined the Fraud Squad, which was in theory a nine to five job, but in practice was eight to eight with his phone next to the bed; he was always scowling intensely, lost deep inside his own importance. He wasn't naturally a computer geek or a maths genius, so he was continually scaling a steep learning curve, but he held up his difficulties as evidence not of his own weakness but as proof of the superior difficulty of the job. If Rose talked about her own work, interviewing heroin addict burglars and wading through disappointing forensic reports, he practically rolled his eyes.

They lived in a flat - they called it an apartment - that they had bought together before their wedding, when they were excited about being so young and smart and up-and-coming. It was in a stylish, modern three-storey block, with carpeted stairs and security coded doors and a corporate shrubbery along the path outside. Inside the apartment the kitchen/living area was open plan, designed for young couples to chat about their day while cooking supper, but of course Rose and Gavin never quite achieved that routine of loosened ties and large glasses of wine and bubbling risotto. Instead, the open plan living area set them against one another when their shifts collided: they were never tired or hungry at the same time, and always in each other's way. Their shared living space felt like an airport, a place of comings and goings, desultory processed food and falling asleep in chairs.

"We were like rats in a trap," Rose said, "bickering all the time, snapping at each other. We could get into a fight over anything. Just the way I squeezed the toothpaste wound him up."

Nick laughed.

"I was just as bad," she confessed. "I found the smallest things about him annoying. Just the way he undid his shoes." She remembered vividly the way Gavin sat ponderously on the sofa to take his shoes off, carefully pinching his trousers as he sat to avoid stretching the knees, and then laboriously untying his laces and tugging them loose; he didn't lift his feet out of the shoes but instead took each shoe off with his hands, bringing the shoes neatly together and carrying them, hooked on two fingers, into the hall, to line up alongside his weekend trainers. He was slow and methodical and utterly superior.

"And then the small arguments would lead on to big arguments," she added. It was like igniting a chain of resentments, touching off inflammatory tapers that were all joined and intertwined. "We were tangled up in bad feeling." Each dispute had an evolutionary tree that stretched right back through their relationship; whatever it was that had brought them together had long since gone extinct.

Nick shook his head. "You can't come back from that," he said. "Sometimes you just have to walk away."

Rose blew out smoke and nodded. "We tried lots of fresh starts," she said, "but the only one that worked was the fresh start without each other."

Nick shifted his foot slightly in the door. In the distance a lorry moaned along the main road. The car park sloped upwards from where they stood, the cars in neat rows reflecting the shine of the high, bright lights; here, by the door, was a ditch of darkness, where the edge of the tarmac had broken up, and the rich, moist crumbs looked almost like soil, sprouting small hardy tufts of grass and a single dandelion. Rose picked idly at the pebbledash wall. She looked vulnerable in the half light, smoking a cigarette like someone taking a break not just from work but from the weight of the mask they wore to face the world. Nick watched her small white fingers digging at the mottled grey wall.

"It was the opposite problem for me and Ellie," he said. "We didn't fight, we didn't get on each other's nerves... we lost interest, basically. Drifted apart. She met someone else."

"Oh, that's harsh."

"Not really. We were already over by then," he explained. "In a way I was pleased for her."

Was he? There was some truth in what he said: when Ellie confessed she had met someone else, part of him had felt relieved, as if a fragile thing he had been forced to carefully carry around with him had finally shattered, and he was free to shrug and walk away.

"I know it's a cliché," he added, "but we got married too young."

It was an easy excuse. The truth was perhaps more complicated, more nuanced, as the truth always is. Nick had loved Ellie - no doubt about it - but somehow, by the time she left him for Christian, he had stopped loving her, and he didn't know when or why it had happened. Somehow they had fallen out of love simply by losing concentration. They didn't talk about it much. Looking back, it was remarkable how little they talked about anything other than the practicalities - money, selling the house, arrangements for the kids - it was as if divorce was the natural next step in the journey of life, and they had both expected to arrive here at some point. Didn't everybody? They congratulated themselves on being civilised, putting the children first, not fighting: they seemed to be on such common ground that their divorce was a joint enterprise, a project undertaken together - and successfully. They made a good team.

Did he feel jealous of Christian? He didn't think so, although he had to admit to a sense of satisfaction when Ellie and Christian fell apart a few years later. He realised then that seeing other people's relationships die was a comfort to him. It was reassuring. Marriage, he believed, was an ill-conceived notion, and couples who said they were happy were lying to themselves, or afraid of being alone. Man's natural state was to be solitary in the world, and since the divorce Nick had indeed remained alone, a realist. He had made himself a nest, and he felt safe.

Rose had finished her cigarette, but she didn't move. They stood together in the night. She was very different from Ellie, he realised, almost an opposite. She was sure of herself in situations where Ellie would wobble, but vulnerable where Ellie would be stout: Ellie was practical, and decisive, but timid outside of her comfort zone, and she had always insisted that she had been "thick" at school. When she worked, she put her shoulders into manual work: cleaning, shelf-stacking, elderly care. Rose was intellectually confident, clever and besuited, but she shimmered with doubt and ambiguity - "a thinking person, not a doing person," Ellie would say, if she met her. Ellie didn't have much patience for thinking people.

"Better get back to it," said Rose.

They both hesitated. There was something in the moment that they didn't want to walk away from, not just yet, but they didn't quite know what to do with it either. Neither of them looked tired any more: the night seemed fresh and alive.

Nick pulled the door open wider, so they could get back in.

"More interviews?" he asked.

"Not just yet," she said, as they stepped into the light. "I've decided to go and visit the scene. Hoping for some inspiration, I guess."

Act Three

The Scene of the Crime

1

Rose sat in the passenger seat of the car, her feet lost in the dark footwell and the streetlights sweeping over her in long slow waves as they drove through the town. Sophie was driving, changing gear smoothly with her graceful, manicured hand. The car was quite new and still carried the acrid smell of factory-fresh plastic and fabric; the air conditioning held them in a perfect bubble, so no-one had ever opened the windows. Sophie paused briefly at the empty roundabout and powered on to the ring road.

Leaving the police station, Rose felt that they were casting adrift, tacking into the dark night, navigating by the sparse and sporadic lights. The landscape of the town was obscured; it was a different place at night. Lit buildings loomed up like towering ships, while the dark park hunkered down, almost invisible. Occasionally they saw another car, fellow travellers who gave no acknowledgement, anonymous behind rushing headlights. On the ring road, as they sailed a long curve around the edge of the town, the scrubland on Rose's left became a black void between the car and the horizon: nothing could be seen.

Sometimes working a night shift made Rose feel sharp and powerful - it felt good to be active while the rest of the world was asleep. But sometimes she felt small and clumsy, and the mass of the sleeping town - so many people, so many lives, so many unknowns -

seemed to hold all the power. She was just fumbling in the darkness.

Sophie slowed for another roundabout, and Rose flicked awake the tablet computer that she held in her lap. "There was nothing useful in the social media, was there?" she said.

"Nothing," replied Sophie. "Just bog standard lifestyle stuff."

The tablet was well-used - even mistreated - and a little senile: it responded only slowly, and occasionally froze in a panic with the lower half of the screen black. Rose coaxed it gently, and scrolled though Facebook. Carl had a page promoting his business, Fine Grooves, but his personal page seemed to be no more than an extension of the business page: he shared music, videos, pictures - northern soul, jazz funk, mod, blue note - there was a whole culture out there, a whole language, and his "friends" were acolytes or customers, leaving enthusiastic comments. Everything linked smoothly with Twitter and Instagram. Rose switched to Georgia's page. Again, the personal was professional: Rose scrolled through a series of motivational memes and stirring images - every post exhorted her to embrace her goals, believe in herself and make every day epic. Georgia's business was fitness as a way of life; fitness as satisfaction for the soul.

Were these personal pages really personal? Carl and Georgia had carefully crafted their Facebook personas. Even posts which appeared intimate or confessional had a professional polish about them, an uber-positive edge. But wasn't that how everyone painted themselves? What else did Rose expect to find? She had no way into the hearts and minds of these people.

"They were a very successful couple, weren't they?" she observed. "White teeth, label clothes, money."

"They were go-getters," agreed Sophie. "Ambitious. The type who want to win at everything."

"But does that tell us anything?" Rose let the tired tablet rest, and the screen gratefully turned black.

"No," said Sophie. "There are thousands of people like them."

Rose looked out at the night again. They were passing houses, dead-eyed, unlit. Trees looked sinister: uneven black shapes against black gardens. Then streetlights broke over them again, a sequence of warm bursts as they moved forwards, lighting the angles and spaces inside the car. Rose tapped her fingers on the tablet, willing herself to think.

"It's a domestic," she said, finally, with a sigh. "That's what we come back to, don't we, in the end? Wife stabs husband. Matrimonial tension plus alcohol plus hot weather. Why would the McAllisters have done it?"

"We can't rule them out though," replied Sophie. "You can't put too much weight on motive." She paused while she pulled on to the next roundabout. "You taught me that."

Rose laughed. "I taught you something?"

Sophie was smiling. "You taught me everything."

"Take it all with a pinch of salt. I know nothing."

It was true about the motive issue though: Rose had known murder cases with no motive at all, especially ones involving sudden violence. People were capable of killing their own children - or complete strangers - without being able to ever explain why.

"Do you remember Geoffrey Billinghay? Before your time, probably."

"I've heard of him," said Sophie. "Was he one of yours?"

"I was on the team. I was only a DC back then." Geoffrey Billinghay was an ordinary man in his fifties, a gas fitter, divorced many years before, no history of mental illness, no oddness, no apparent problems. One day he just set out from his house with an axe, attacking neighbours and passers-by, people at a bus stop. "He couldn't say why he did it at all - in interview he kept saying 'I suppose I just snapped' - that was all he could say. 'I just snapped', like he'd just, I don't know, shouted at a traffic warden or thrown a cup or something. Luckily Geoffrey's attacks were so half-hearted and haphazard that no-one was killed - after swinging at one person he'd move straight on to the next, as if he had the whole world to get through - but there were some serious injuries. They got a psychiatric report for the trial but they couldn't find anything wrong with him. I think we were all hoping there'd be some sort of psychosis or something, some explanation."

"It's not nice to accept that someone sane can just go off the rails," said Sophie.

"It makes everyone a potential murderer," agreed Rose.

"You sound like Hal," Sophie grinned.

Rose laughed. "I know," she said, "that's Hal: trust no-one. Everyone's a suspect. Even your own grandmother."

They passed a supermarket, brightly lit with yellow light. The broad car park was empty. It looked strange:

in the daytime this car park was overstuffed, with cars jostling in queues and fighting for spaces.

"I don't want to speak out of turn," said Sophie, slowly, "but, you know, you should probably be a bit wary of Hal."

"What?"

"I mean, I'm sorry, I probably shouldn't say this." Sophie's eyes were on the road. "Honestly, tell me if I'm speaking out of turn."

"No... go on." Rose had no idea where this was going.

"It's just... look: I'll be frank, okay? I know you're watching out for Butland, and I can see why, believe me, he's as slimy as anything, all that creeping up to the DCI, going behind your back, but you know, he's kind of obvious, really. Everyone can see what he's like. And he's lazy, everyone knows that, he'll never get anywhere. The DCI doesn't like him." She took a breath, still looking at the road. "It's Hal you should be careful of. I mean, he's friendly and all smiles, he's a lovely guy, but he's ambitious. He doesn't want to be your right hand man forever. He's the type that wants to learn from you and then pass you. You know?"

Rose didn't know what to say.

"I'm sorry," said Sophie. "I shouldn't be saying all this..."

"No, it's okay..."

"I'm speaking out of turn."

"No, it's fine. Thank you. It's okay." Rose paused. "It's okay, I know Hal's ambitious. But thank you."

There was a silence.

"We're nearly there," said Sophie. "It's just off Green Avenue, isn't it?"

"That's right."

The car turned into Green Avenue, and moved steadily up a gentle slope. Before this area was developed for housing, there were fields and meadows, and the streets had been named in tribute: Buttercup Close, Foxglove Drive, Riverside View. There was a river out there somewhere, on the other side of the hill they were climbing, in the valley that was still dark and wild, skulking at the edge of the expanding town. Sophie was slowing down for the next turning.

Her comments - more than comments, Rose thought: it was a little speech, a planned speech - had thrown Rose off course; she didn't like to think about office politics - the jostling, the competition - the unpleasant complications of the workplace. To do their job well, they had to work as a team, and yet there were appraisals and reviews and re-organisations; roles to be applied for; roles that disappeared; promotions; training programmes; advancements and displacements. It was as if the job itself was day-to-day life, but the 'career' was the ground beneath Rose's feet, the thing that she gave little thought to, but which could unexpectedly and seismically shift or change at any time.

She had always trusted Hal; she considered him a friend. She was one of the few people who knew he was gay; while not exactly a secret, it was something you were discreet about in this job, in this town. She had always trusted Sophie too; but it unsettled her to realise that Sophie had been giving so much thought to the politics of the team, the machinations and future possibilities, the way 'the game' would play out. It saddened Rose, this inescapable undertow of competition in life. It had been there even in childhood, even in family life: look how clever your brother is, look how pretty your sister is. Gavin had embraced it, even enjoyed it - he had encouraged her to apply for training programmes, to make contacts, to network and to make herself visible to the senior staff - perhaps, since her divorce, she had taken her eye off the ball.

But was she really ambitious? Did she really care? Thinking about her career, an uncomfortable question came to Rose: was she running towards something, or running away from something else? If she pictured herself as a DCI, she just saw herself as older, dowdier, earning a bit more money and attending meetings instead of handling cases… nothing about the picture excited her. It was another rung up the ladder, but what was the point of that? She would still just be standing on a ladder.

Perhaps the only reason she wanted success was because she didn't want to be seen as a failure. She didn't want to be old and grey and answering to younger, smarter superiors. She didn't want to become part of the furniture, someone who had been in the CID office forever, heading up a team of faces that came and went, surpassing her. She didn't want to be like those guys who never made it past sergeant, who grew fat drinking tea with two sugars and talking about their gardens and caravan holidays.

Thinking about sergeants made her think of Nick - but he was different, a custody sergeant, master of his own domain, a specialist. Thinking of Nick, she felt a little jolt in her stomach, and worried that she had blushed when she spoke to him earlier. When she was young her skin had always given her away. Had anyone noticed her and Nick together and thought anything of it? Just two smokers, outside the back door… she should be careful. The police station craved gossip like a sponge craves water. But she found herself smiling. She wasn't wrong, was she? There was a connection between them, a warmth, a spark, whatever you want to call it. They liked each other. Would anything come of it?

"This is it," said Sophie, and turned the car into Riverside View.

It was a cul-de-sac, formed in a long L-shape, the houses built ten or fifteen years ago, new but not brand new. There were streetlights, and gardens, and everywhere the detritus of suburbia: children's bicycles, paddling pools, trampolines, mid-size cars doubled up on short driveways, mown lawns, flower beds, wheelie bins decorated with stickers and tucked tidily into corners. Most of the houses were in darkness, so number nine was easy to spot from the lit windows downstairs and the police car outside - there was also police tape strung loosely around the boundary, wrapped around a lamppost and a bin. The forensic team had gone, and just one officer sat in his car, guarding the house and playing with his phone. He looked up at their approach and sat up straighter.

"It's pretty much what we imagined," Sophie said. "Middle class suburbia."

"Ordinary lives," agreed Rose, as the car came to a stop.

Of course, she reflected, before climbing out, her career was an escape route from her mother, or so she hoped. Perhaps that was her real motivation. If she moved up to DCI, she would almost certainly have to move to another town where there was a vacancy, perhaps even to another force in another region. But would she really escape her mother? There would be telephone calls, doleful requests for visits. "We're both on our own, Rose," she'd say, stoically. "We have to be there for each other."

Sophie killed the engine.

"Right then," said Rose. "Let's have a look around."

2

Back at the custody desk, Nick was under electric light, halfway through his shift, sipping a half mug of cold tea. He had set Aaron to heating up food for the Lewis boys, who had been complaining, and he could hear the microwave whirring and pinging in the kitchen behind him. The officers dealing with the case, Ash and Kyle, had disappeared again. He had checked on Brian Dunn, and found him curled up asleep on the floor of his cell with his blanket happily clasped under his chin. His breathing was normal and he was lying on his side, so Nick left him there. Katrina had gone to fetch Alice from her cell so PC Whealdon could interview her. Nick was able to mentally tick every name on his whiteboard - he knew where they were, knew they were safe, and knew what was happening to them next. The back door buzzed and he could see PC Lasky on his monitor. He let him in.

Katrina came back through at that moment. Setting down his cold tea, Nick intercepted her. "Hey," he said quietly. "I didn't get a chance to ask; how's Stuart?"

Katrina paused. Her expression didn't change. "He's not good," she said at last. "I really shouldn't be working."

"Do you need to take the rest of the shift off?"

She hesitated, one hand on the custody desk, looking at her hand and not meeting Nick's eyes. They both knew Nick would struggle to find another custodian to come in and take over. As they stood in uncertain silence, PC Lasky came in, jangling his car keys. "Bad news for Alan Stamper, I'm afraid," he announced as he came up to the desk. "His wife wants to press charges."

Katrina moved away. "She's been down to A&E," PC Lasky went on, "and she's had stitches, just two, but you know… she's got her sister there, her neighbours there, they're all carrying on. They've thrown half his stuff out into the front garden. They're like a lynch mob."

"She's made a statement then?"

"She certainly has. He's gone too far this time. I'm going to have to interview him and probably charge him."

Aaron was carrying a tray of microwaved curry, wobbling as he went, so Nick went to fetch Alan Stamper from his cell. He had been asleep, and he smelled bad. He rose, a tall man unsteady on his feet, rubbing his hollow face with both hands. Ungainly, he limped like a grey-muzzled old wolf as he followed Nick into the corridor, half-awake, looking like he might stumble at any moment. "Can I go home now, boss?" he asked.

"Need to ask you a few questions first," said Nick.

"Can I have a cup of tea?"

"I'll get you one in a minute."

PC Lasky was standing outside the interview room, holding the door, and Alan realised what was happening. He stopped before the doorway like a stubborn horse. "What the fuck?"

"Calm down, Alan," said Nick.

"I'm getting interviewed? That bitch is carrying on with this bullshit?" He swung round and started gesturing with his long arms. "It's her you should be interviewing! I want to make a fucking complaint against her…"

"Calm down, Alan," repeated Nick, with his palms up, shepherding him towards the interview room. "Just sit down and we'll sort all this out." He and PC Lasky approached Alan as they would a wild animal, with steady movements and clear instructions. "Just go in and sit down and I'll get you a cup of tea."

"Fuck this," said Alan.

"Come on," said PC Lasky. "You know the score. She's got two stitches in her face."

"She fucking started it!"

"You can tell me all that in the interview. Don't make this worse for yourself…"

"Fuck this!"

"You know the score, Alan," repeated PC Lasky. "You've overstepped the mark this time, you've got to accept the consequences. You've made your own bed…"

"Fuck," said Alan, again, but he suddenly jerked his twitchy body into the room and sat heavily and angrily on the bench, in furious surrender. PC Lasky followed him in and Nick shut the door on them, relieved.

Some people, he reflected as he walked back to his desk, lived their whole lives at a fever pitch. Alan Stamper and his wife were the kind of people who were constantly screaming at one another, drinking cheap lager, throwing things, their neighbours bawling at them to shut up, Alan squaring up to everyone; it seemed an exhausting way to live. Alan's life was one endless drama, always on the edge of violence. Nick thought of his own peaceful home: the silence, the order, the restfulness.

Nick lived alone, and had done ever since his divorce. He had lived alone before, too, when he was a student, many years ago, before he and Ellie got married. The two periods of solitary life were very different though: a young man living alone is different from a middle aged man living alone. A young man alone is swollen with future, right at the start of things, a kaleidoscope of possibilities shifting in him from moment to moment. He can be messy and rampant - life is like one long preparation for a night out. Food can be disposable junk, a bed can be a mattress on the floor, a stereo can sit on top of a crate and clothes can rest where they fall. A young man can drink too much and smoke too much and make mistakes like confetti. If a middle aged man is messy, though, if he drinks or smokes or eats takeaways every night, the meaning is the opposite - dark and degenerate - life is one long hangover, one long morning after. The unwashed dishes and unwashed clothes are like so many regrets and defeats. A middle aged man has to be neat and clean, in control of his possessions, purposeful in his routines. He has to live irreproachably.

What about an old man living alone? Nick hadn't considered that picture before... he could only imagine a shrunken, frugal life, in front of a single bar electric fire. He shook the image from his head. He liked his house, his habits, his clean fridge and orderly laundry.

He had to admit, though, that the interlude of living as part of a family had been joyful at times; in fact, he couldn't say that he had really been unhappy much, if at all. Life was messy and often frustrating, but it was also warm and satisfying: children in pyjamas watching cartoons, toys scattered in the garden, hamsters scratching in a cage. Ellie had accused him of never being fully there, of dipping in and out, of rushing off to work whenever life at home got hard. Perhaps that was true. He hadn't been involved enough with the children. Often Ellie had to translate for him - "She doesn't like that story any more" she would say, or "He's embarrassed when you do that." But… it might not be too late. It would be nice, he thought, if Joe came to visit regularly; maybe it could become a Sunday thing, the two of them together, hanging out at Nick's place. Maybe even over the summer they could do some kind of hobby together - embark on a project - what did fathers and sons do? Nick could picture them together, in his kitchen, eating bacon butties and planning something, although he couldn't quite imagine what, not yet.

They had discussed destiny, that Sunday afternoon, when they were talking about *Macbeth*. The three witches in the play made prophecies, and the prophecies came true, exactly as they said: Macbeth became Thane of Cawdor, and then King. They could see into the future; did that mean that fate exists, and the future is already written? "But," Joe said, "Macbeth *makes* it all come true. You could say they're manipulating him - they tell him he'll become king, so he sets about making it happen. Look, here, he says - " Joe read the words from the book awkwardly, a modern teenager intoning Elizabethan English " - 'If chance will make me king, why, chance may crown me, without my stir' - but actually he *does* stir, he commits all these murders to make himself king, he makes the prophecy come true. So maybe what Shakespeare is really telling us is that we're all in charge of our own destiny. There's no fate. *We* make stuff happen."

A powerful idea for a sixteen-year-old, Nick had thought at the time: you are in charge of your own destiny. Joe was so young, with so much time and possibility that Nick was awed at the thought of him taking control of his own future, and making it happen. But now it struck him that it was a powerful idea for a fortysomething too. His own destiny wasn't written; his future was in his own hands. There was no prophecy.

He thought then of Rose, and that cigarette break earlier, that intimate conversation... he wasn't wrong, was he? There was something between them, something they could take hold of if they wanted to. The thought made his stomach flip. Nerves, excitement, fear? All of those.

A commotion in the corridor brought his thoughts back to work. PC Whealdon had come out of his interview room with Alice, and she was upset.

"Come on, please," she was crying. "Come on, I haven't done anything. I didn't touch the bike - have you got my fingerprints on it? Come on..."

PC Whealdon was shaking his head and avoiding her eyes.

"Katrina!" called Nick. "Can you take Alice back to her cell?"

Alice now came up to the custody desk to appeal directly to Nick.

"Sergeant, come on, you can see I haven't done anything wrong... I was just in the wrong place at the wrong time, that's all."

Katrina gently took her arm. Alice, still crying, tried to shake her off. Her arm looked as brittle and bony as a twig, her elbow sticking sharply out of her baggy t-shirt. She was angry now, quite suddenly, wriggling and stamping, and she reminded Nick of his own teenage daughter, Lucy: tearful one minute, tough the next. Alice, though, lived in a different, far more dangerous world. Nick had seen her in and out of custody for years. She must have been only twelve or thirteen when she first started getting into trouble. She seemed to always be alone, a waif. She was shouting now, but Katrina was leading her away easily, as if she had no more power than a rag doll. Nick could hear her complaining all the way to her cell.

"They can't even get their stories straight," said PC Whealdon, settling his arms comfortably on top of the desk. "They're a pair of comedians, they are."

"What have they said?" asked Nick. He picked up his mug, looked at the cold tea, and decided to finally abandon it. He must remember to make one for Alan Stamper.

"Well," began PC Whealdon. He liked to tell a story. "Jerome, he says he was just walking along minding his own business when someone he knows only casually came up to him with this bike and asked him to look after it. This individual is someone he knows only as Digger - yes, Digger, he doesn't know his real name of course, and what does he look like? Oh, just ordinary, you know, average height, average hair, no distinguishing features at all. So this Digger asks Jerome to look after a bike for him, in the middle of the night, no reasons given, no plan to meet up later to return it... Jerome sees nothing suspicious about this - must happen to him all the time - so he wanders off, pushing this bike, not going anywhere in particular. And the tools in his bag? Well, yes, he says, they *are* his tools, and he's got them because he's arranged to do some work for a mate in the morning, and he was going to stay at another mate's house overnight and go straight there so he brought the tools with him... the mate's name? Oh, he's rather not say. The mate's address? Oh no, he doesn't want to involve anyone. Going equipped? The very idea! He doesn't break into places, well, not any more. He just had his tools to do an honest day's work... what kind of work? Well, um, fixing up his mate's shed. Oh, and Alice? Yes, she was just with him; they were just out for a stroll."

PC Whealdon took a breath.

"Then we get to Alice's story. She's just out for a walk, you know, late at night, and she bumps into Jerome, and walks with him for a bit, having a chat, and then he says he has to pick up this bike. She thinks nothing of it, nothing suspicious, and she just waits at the gate of this unknown house while he goes into the garden... shed burglary? The very idea! Was she a lookout? Of course not! Why would she think anything suspicious was going on? After a while Jerome comes out of the garden wheeling this bike... nothing suspicious about that, is there? And Jerome's tools... yes, she says, she might have touched them, her prints might be on them because - are you ready for this? - Jerome wanted to show them to her. They just stopped in the middle of the street and he got out his screwdriver and his hammer to show them to her. But she didn't touch the bike - oh, she's adamant about that. And no, she's never heard of anyone called Digger."

PC Whealdon slapped the desk. "So, what do you think, Serge? Enough to charge?"

Nick nodded. "Charge them both with going equipped to steal and burglary of the shed. They can probably do a deal in court, but for now we'll charge both of them with both offences."

PC Whealdon nodded. "I'll do the charge sheets."

Katrina had come quietly up to the desk.

"Problem?" asked Nick.

Katrina pulled a face. "I'm a bit worried about Georgia Lane."

Nick gave her a questioning look.

"She's gone really quiet. I mean, *really* quiet. I know the doctor gave her a sedative but, I don't know, she's being weird…"

Nick was nodding. "I'll come down and talk to her. Maybe we should put her on fifteen minute checks. Would you be able to cover that?"

Katrina nodded. In the corridor, they could hear Alan Stamper coming out of his interview room. "This is bullshit!" he was shouting. "I want to make a complaint!"

3

The forensic team had finished with the kitchen, and the room was left just as it was, taped off, like a diorama in a museum. Rose and Sophie stepped carefully. There was blood on the floor, smeared by many footprints, and random flecks and smudges of red on the table and cupboards; there was a sense of the panic and activity that had taken place here. Now it was silent and the blood had dried.

The kitchen was, incongruously, a cheerful room: there were cartons of breakfast cereal, colourful mugs, matching jars for tea and coffee. On the table there was a glass and a chopping board and lemons and limes still innocently waiting, some neatly sliced and drying up. Just one glass, Rose noticed, used but empty. Carl's glass?

It was shocking to think that a man had been murdered here, in this ordinary kitchen, by a killer who used an ordinary kitchen knife - nothing dangerous or exotic, nothing bought for a nefarious purpose, just a knife used to chop fruit, a knife that could preposterously kill a man with one movement, one stab into his vulnerable throat. It would have taken seconds; no, less than a second. Rose looked at the floor. Did he know, as he lay there, that he was dying? He must have lain there, on his own kitchen floor, in his own house, in shock and disbelief. He must have felt pain, confusion, and his own warm blood vomiting out of him. What thoughts went through his mind?

The question Rose had to answer was who, but surely the real question was why. Why did this man die? A young, happy man, wiped out by the single action of a single moment, by a weapon that was never meant to be a weapon, in a room that was never meant to be a murder scene. A sunny Sunday at home should be the safest place in the world - why had this aberration occurred? How did it make sense?

Rose had dealt with murder cases before, but the victims had usually lived violent lives: they were men who went out fighting, boys who carried knives, women who knew they were in danger but couldn't escape. They were people who lived close to death, like soldiers on a battlefield; that was their world. That didn't mean that Rose wasn't sorry for them - on the contrary, she wished that they could have been lifted out of that world before they were crushed - but the fact was it was a different world, a dark, violent world, an alternative existence.

Carl Lane, though, had lived in the ordinary world, Rose's world. He had a nice house, a successful business, an inspiring Facebook profile. He had had every reason to believe that his kitchen knife was just a kitchen knife, not a weapon that would be used to kill him.

Perhaps the two worlds were not separate after all.

"Shall we look at the garden?" said Sophie.

Rose nodded. The back door, UPVC with a frosted glass panel, was unlocked. The garden was dark, lit and shadowed by the light from the kitchen window. There was a tall fence hiding it from the view of the neighbours. Even in the dark, Rose could see that it was a tidily kept garden, the small lawn mown and the shrubs trimmed, and the large patio was furnished like a room, with a chiminea, solid table and cushioned chairs, candles that had guttered out, a cold heater, and a brick barbecue, the charcoal laid out but not lit. There were three glasses on the table, each still containing liquid and pieces of lime, a dead fly floating in one of them. It seemed that only Carl had taken his drink inside. Rose looked back at the house. The kitchen window could be seen from the patio, and at night, ablaze with light and with the blind up, part of the interior of the kitchen was visible, though at an angle; it would not be so easy to see in on a sunny afternoon. The patio was nearer to the door than the window, but the glass in the door was obscured so that only a blur of yellow light could be seen.

"Any thoughts?" said Rose. Her voice was quiet under the vast starlit sky.

Sophie's hair shone even in the dark. She was looking carefully at everything. "Nothing contradicts anything any of them have said." She looked across at Rose. "Unfortunately."

They went back into the kitchen, and stepped carefully around the blood on the floor.

"It's a sturdy door," Rose said. "But anyone in the garden would probably hear raised voices or screams, even if it was closed. If it was open, they should have heard any argument, although of course couples can argue very discreetly if they know they could be overheard…" She felt this was going nowhere. Her eyes travelled the kitchen worktops. "That's a bit odd," she said.

It was a seven inch record, in its sleeve, lying flat on the kitchen worktop in front of a spice rack. Rose stepped closer to look at it without picking it up. The cover showed a black and white photograph of American police officers standing over a man on the ground; people holding placards, at some sort of protest, were in the background. " 'The Rolling Stones - Street Fighting Man,' " Rose read out. "It's old - Sixties, probably. Maybe he'd just picked it up from somewhere? Although Georgia said they went to B&Q that morning - he wasn't visiting record fairs or anything. I wonder why it's in the kitchen."

Sophie was already googling the title on her phone. "This is interesting," she said. "It was banned in America because of anti-Vietnam War protests - it was seen as inflammatory..." She paused, scrolling down. "Hey, it's really valuable - with that sleeve. They changed the cover... that must be the original US release, with the picture of police violence at a protest." She tapped at her phone excitedly. "Wow... it's worth a lot. We're talking thousands. Lots of thousands."

Rose looked down at the picture. The cardboard sleeve was in good condition for something that must have been fifty years old. "So why is it here?" she asked. "Why was something that valuable left out in the kitchen, where it could get wet? Carl and Georgia were tidy people... he must have brought it in here and put it down there for a reason."

"To sell to someone? Someone who was coming round?"

"Maybe. It could be a sign that someone else was coming to the house." Rose paused. "We should definitely fingerprint it."

Sophie came forward expertly with an evidence bag and used a pen to slide the record off the worktop. Rose watched her. "It's funny, isn't it?" she said. "Something so valuable just because it's rare. There's nothing intrinsically valuable about it. You could probably download the song for next to nothing."

"That was Carl's whole business," said Sophie. "Rarity." She sealed the bag. "Do you think maybe this gives weight to the intruder story? Maybe a thief was disturbed?"

Rose considered. "Maybe. Has anyone checked upstairs?"

They looked at each other.

"Butland didn't mention it," said Sophie. "He didn't notice this record, either."

"We'd better take a look. We need to go up anyway, to check out Georgia's story - to see how likely it is that she spent that long fixing her hair and makeup and didn't hear her husband being murdered downstairs."

Sophie nodded. There was a light on in the hall, but the upstairs was entirely in darkness. Rose flicked the switches until the landing light came on.

"You don't think -" Sophie said suddenly. She lowered her voice. "If there *was* an intruder, he could still be hiding up there, avoiding all the coming and going."

Rose paused. "It's unlikely, but you're right to be careful. Stay alert."

Climbing the stairs, she felt unexpectedly nervous, although she was fairly sure that any intruder would have made his escape by now. As a detective inspector, it wasn't often that she was in physically dangerous situations. She remembered her younger days, in training, when she did beat work: outside nightclubs where people were throwing up, arriving at the scene of street fights with her hand on her canister of CS gas, rushing into the middle of confrontations between neighbours or drivers or couples. She had never been injured, but once a beer bottle had been thrown and hit her shoulder, miraculously without breaking. The raw violence of it had made her feel vulnerable, but she had her training to rely on: procedures, guidelines and protocols were comforting. Although every situation was unique and unpredictable, it was useful to have plans - numbered steps to go through to tame the wild messiness of life.

That was how her ex-husband, Gavin, had approached the whole of his life, she reflected: he always followed a predetermined procedure. Perhaps he took it too far - he was perhaps a little too inflexible. He had a plan for his career and he stuck to it. He planned his hobbies, researching the right equipment, joining clubs, seeking out instructions. He had decided he didn't want children, and had a prepared speech about overpopulation that he delivered to anyone who questioned him. He reviewed his pension arrangements every five years.

During all the time they were together, he never changed his mind about anything.

Rose reached the top of the stairs. There were four doors, all pulled close but not completely shut, all dark within. "Stay alert," she repeated to Sophie, and then, just in case, she called out: "Police! Come out now!"

The house remained silent.

The master bedroom was at the front, the windows overlooking the silent road. The curtains were open, because of course no-one had made it to bed that night. Rose flicked on the light. The room was decorated beautifully in silver and blue, with co-ordinated fabrics and throw cushions, modern and stylish. There was a white dressing table, hung with patchwork hearts and a dainty chain of fairy lights looped over and around the mirror. Georgia's makeup was spread out but orderly, and her jewellery was arranged on a delicate little ceramic tree. Her hairbrush, dryer and straighteners were lined up like tools at one end of the table. Rose caught sight of herself in the mirror: a serious-faced policewoman in a dark suit, a stranger in a private space who could only be there because of a calamity.

The next bedroom was very small and smelled like a spare room, decorated in white with a very smooth bed; there were some coloured weights on the floor and a pile of storage tubs. The bedroom at the back, overlooking the garden, was where Carl operated his business. It was shelved from floor to ceiling, a grotto of vinyl records, some in rows packed in with alphabetical dividers, some in cases; there was a small desk, on top of which was a laptop, switched off but plugged in to charge. Like every room in the house, it was spotless and neat; Rose, herself quite untidy, was almost alarmed at the perfection of Carl and Georgia's organisation. They were not the kind of people who would ever lose their keys.

The bathroom was beautiful too, of course, white with silver and grey tiles. It had no window, and Rose noticed at once that the light pull automatically switched on a fan, which made an electric whirring sound.

"Listen," she said, and they both stood still. "That's quite loud. It is feasible that if Georgia was in here she might not have heard a commotion downstairs."

"She would have been in the bedroom, though, for most of the time she says she was upstairs," said Sophie. "She's got a mirror in there, and that's where her makeup is, and her hairbrush."

"And," added Rose, stepping out onto the landing, "to walk between the bedroom and the bathroom she would have been right at the top of the steps. The kitchen's just below." She switched off the light and the fan spluttered into silence.

"If the McAllisters had any sort of row with Carl, you would have thought she would have heard something."

Rose nodded and looked back into the bedroom. "She was just sitting there, brushing her hair."

"And they were murdering him downstairs."

"It seems unlikely."

"Unless they planned it. Waited until Georgia went to the loo, then crept in and stabbed him before he could react."

They both stood at the top of the steps, thinking.

Rose sighed. "Anything's possible. If Georgia killed him, that happened quickly too - Annette said there was a bit of an argument but they weren't in the kitchen together for long. Whatever happened, there was no big scene, no long build up." She paused. "Do you think this house is *too* neat?"

Sophie smiled. "It is compared to mine."

"I mean, do you think they were a bit... repressed? I don't want to get all amateur psychologist here but maybe they were a bit buttoned-down, a bit too obsessed with success, a bit too focussed on perfection - maybe Georgia snapped?"

Sophie nodded. "Maybe it was all a facade, a mask - maybe deep down she wanted to smash it all. It's possible."

Rose was looking at the wall at the top of the stairs. She frowned. "Can you see that?"

She stepped forward and moved her head from side to side, trying to get a better look at the mark on the wall. The wallpaper was patterned - tiny silvery swirls on an ivory background - but there was definitely a large stain there, a splash of some sort, at head height, possibly scrubbed but still discernible. Rose ran her hand over the wall. At the top of the stain there was a definite dent.

"A glass thrown at the wall?" she suggested.

Sophie was moving her head around too. The light reflected off all the walls and it was hard to see. "It's definitely a liquid," she agreed. "Like someone threw a glass or a cup of coffee or something."

"It would leave a brown mark if it was tea or coffee," Rose said. "Or if it was blood - if it was someone's head that made the dent... this was a clear liquid, water or white wine or vodka maybe."

"An accident?"

"The cup or glass was thrown with some force to dent the plaster." Rose was right up against it now, sniffing. There was no smell. "It's completely dry," she said. "I don't think it's happened in the last twenty-four hours... but we don't really know." She pulled a face. "Could have happened yesterday, could have happened a year ago. Could be an accident. Could be a sign that they had violent rows. It's something to put to Georgia."

She stepped back from the wall. "I guess we're done here."

They walked back down the stairs. In the hall, a display of photographs in jaunty frames looked out at them eagerly: Georgia and Carl surfing, Georgia and Carl hiking, Georgia and Carl raising their glasses in a bar. They were fit, active, energetic people: did they fight physically behind closed doors? Rose remembered her own arguments with Gavin. They bickered persistently, but neither of them had much of a temper - they never stepped up a gear, as some couples did. Their arguments went round and round, under the pretence that they were getting somewhere, that they could resolve something.

Rose hesitated in the hall, looking again into the brightly lit kitchen. "So Georgia says she came in, and went upstairs, leaving Carl cutting up fruit in here, and the McAllisters in the garden. Think of it as daytime - a hot, sunny afternoon, everyone a bit tipsy. Georgia went upstairs - she may or may not have shut the door between the kitchen and the hall. She used the loo in the bathroom, where there's a noisy fan, but then she went into the quiet bedroom to fix her hair and makeup. The bedroom is up there - not above the kitchen. She heard no arguments, nothing. She came back downstairs - still not hearing any commotion - and walked into the kitchen to find the McAllisters had stabbed Carl in the neck. The question is, is it believable that she heard nothing? And why would they do it?"

"These houses have walls like paper," said Sophie. "If she is telling the truth, there can't have been a row or a fight."

"There were no signs of a struggle," said Rose. "He was taken by surprise. Why would the McAllisters have done that? If they planned to kill him for some reason, there are better ways. They could have come on a weekday when he was alone, and made it look like a burglary... This was definitely a spontaneous killing."

"Maybe it was Annette," Sophie suggested. "Maybe she had a thing for him. Maybe she was a bit drunk and made a move on him, and he rebuffed her. Maybe she felt humiliated and angry and stabbed him, and then Jack came in and covered up for her."

"Maybe." Rose nodded. "Maybe. I wish we had more than speculation."

"Then there's this," said Sophie, holding up the seven inch single in the evidence bag. "What does this mean?"

"It might not mean anything," Rose sighed. She rubbed her eyes. "Let's get back to the office."

4

Kyle and Ash had returned again, reluctantly, to deal with the four youths they had arrested in the stolen car, and they were now slouched over Nick's desk. They had printed out their statements, and Nick was trying to make sense of them.

"So who was the one in the grey hoodie?" he said.

"Drew Beardsley," said Kyle.

"And the one in the red cap?"

"Alfie Lewis, I think."

"You think."

"Well, he's wearing a white cap now, and Stan's wearing the red cap, but I don't know. Ash thought one of the others was wearing the red cap in the back of the car, didn't you Ash?"

Ash nodded.

"Did you put that in your statement?" asked Nick.

Ash looked blank.

"Your statement," Nick said, exasperated. "It's word for word the same as Kyle's."

Ash still looked blank.

"A defence lawyer will have a field day with that," explained Nick. "It looks like you wrote your statements together. Look, we'll just charge them all with TWOC. We can't be sure who was driving."

Kyle and Ash looked disappointed.

Nick looked beyond them to where PC Lasky was waiting.

"Are you ready to charge Alan?"

PC Lasky nodded. "We need to talk about bail," he said, coming forward as Kyle and Ash shuffled away. "Obviously he can't go home, and there's a danger of him going back to threaten her if he's released to any other address in town."

"You think I should remand him in custody?"

PC Lasky shrugged. "He's suggesting his brother's address in Raynall. That's twenty miles away."

"So, if I bailed him there with a condition not to go within two miles of his home address…"

PC Lasky shrugged again. "It's a risk."

"I could give him a bail condition to sign on at Raynall Police Station three times a day. That should keep him there."

"That might work."

"Then again…" Nick pondered. It might be safest to keep Alan in the cells overnight and let the magistrates take responsibility for him in the morning. On the other hand, the cells were pretty busy.

"Are you talking about me, boss?" Alan was out in the corridor - PC Lasky had left him on the bench - and now he came limping up to the desk, adopting a humble, beseeching approach. "Please, boss," he began, " just let me go to my brother's. He'll have me. I won't come back here except for court - I won't cause any trouble. Honest. I know she doesn't want to see me. You can check my record, boss - I've never breached bail before, not for years, anyway. My brother'd come and pick me up - you ring him, you talk to him, he's a good bloke, never been in trouble, he's got a good job and that, he'll straighten me out."

"I don't know if I can trust you, Alan…"

"I don't even have a car! I couldn't come back here if I wanted to... my brother'll pick me up and he'll bring me over for court, you just ring him. You can trust him."

PC Lasky handed over a phone number scrawled on a piece of paper.

"Okay," said Nick, but as he reached for the phone it rang. He put it to his ear.

"Custody."

"Nick, is that you?"

It took him a moment to place the voice. It was out of context, here: it wasn't a work voice. He hesitated.

"Nick?"

"Yes." He realised it was Ellie, his ex-wife.

"It's me, Ellie, I'm sorry to ring you at work like this but Joe said you were on duty tonight" - her voice was worried, urgent, furtive, tumbling - "and it's just that Lucy's gone off somewhere, I don't know where, she stormed off out, I don't know what to do."

"Slow down." Nick moved back from the desk, gripping the phone tightly. "Say that again."

"It's Lucy - we had a bit of a fight earlier because she wanted to go out and I said no - she's been playing up - I think it's because of Joe's exams or the hot weather, I don't know - anyway, we had this fight and then she wouldn't get ready for bed, so I just left her, and then she came out of her bedroom again and we had another big row..."

Alan was trying to get Nick's attention, and Nick had to turn away, pressing the phone to his ear as if he could carry this conversation in a tiny bubble of privacy. He was prickling with fear.

"...she just stormed off out; I thought she'd come straight back, you know, I thought she'd just stomp once round the block and get scared and come home, but she hasn't, and I've rung Alysha's house but she's not been there."

"What time did she go?"

"Oh God, it was ages ago now, just after midnight..."

"That's hours ago!"

"I can't go out after her - Joe's asleep upstairs, he's got an exam tomorrow - and honestly, I don't know where to start looking." Her voice was brittle, on the edge of tears. "I can't think where she would be if she's not at Alysha's. And she didn't take her phone with her - she left it here, in her bedroom. Oh God."

"Try ringing all her friends," Nick said. He was trying to stay calm. He could deal with this; he dealt with crises all the time, every day; it was his job. But this was his family, his real life. He thought of Lucy, out there somewhere in the night, untethered, and it was hard to breathe. "Ring everyone - her friends, friends of friends - get more numbers from everyone you ring. I'll get some bobbies out looking for her."

"Should we report her as missing?"

A missing child. Nick thought about social workers, registers, school notifications, the kids who turned up again and again in his cells. "No, I'll do it unofficially," he said. "What was she wearing?"

"Um, black leggings, trainers, and that Superdry jacket."

Nick didn't know the jacket. He realised he didn't see his daughter very often. "What colour's the jacket?"

"Green, a sort of khaki green, a camouflage green."

"But not patterned?"

"No."

"Okay."

Alan was pleading loudly with PC Lasky now.

"I'll get on to it," said Nick. "You get ringing all her friends. Everyone you can think of."

He came off the phone. The room seemed very bright and busy, and his mind felt full to bursting.

"Will you ring him, boss?"

Nick took the piece of paper from PC Lasky with the telephone number scribbled on it. "Yes, yes I will, I'll think about bail, Alan, but I need you to go back in your cell while I think."

"But boss, you just have to ring…"

Aaron came floating by at that moment and Nick almost grabbed him physically. "Aaron! Can you put Alan back in his cell for me please?"

"Boss, please…"

Aaron led Alan away and Nick turned to PC Lasky. "Can I ask a favour?"

"Sure." PC Lasky looked surprised at the fervour of Nick's tone.

"That was my ex-wife on the phone. She says my daughter's stormed out after an argument and she hasn't come home. She's only fourteen. Could you go out and drive around and look for her?"

"Uh, yeah, sure…"

"She lives on Bramwell Street, near the high school. If you could start around there… she's got brown hair, quite long, and she's not very tall, she's slim…" Small, he was thinking, she's so small. "She's wearing a green jacket, a sort of camo green."

"Okay." PC Lasky was looking at him curiously. "Don't worry, mate. Teenagers do this all the time."

"I know." Nick realised how flushed and anxious he looked, and tried to slow down. It was his job to always be calm; he liked to think of himself as unflappable. "I'd just be grateful if you'd go out and look for her."

PC Lasky nodded and set off. Kyle was standing in the doorway.

"Are you ready to charge these lads now, Serge?" he asked.

"Uh, yes." Nick was still holding the piece of paper with Alan's brother's number on it. Everything suddenly seemed too much. He wanted to run out into the night to look for his daughter.

"Shall we get them out of their cells?"

"Yes. No! We'll need the Lewis boys' mother here for charge - where did she go?"

Kyle looked blank.

"Get her. And a social worker for Drew. And find out if any of them are already on bail for anything else."

Kyle stood looking at him. Nick was replaying PC Lasky's words in his head: *teenagers do this all the time*. Nick's daughter didn't. His family were not part of this world. He took a breath and then snapped at Kyle: "Get on with it!"

5

"Hal's found something," called Butland, as Rose and Sophie walked into the CID room.

Although the room was brightly lit, there was something about it that made Rose think of a cave: it was perhaps the suspended ceiling, the off-white, soft-textured tiles overhead that made the room long and low. It was a warm room, too, stuffy and still. Butland was lounging at his desk and grinning. Hal was sitting upright at his computer.

"How did it go?" he asked Rose, looking up.

Rose and Sophie came across the room and pulled chairs up to Hal's desk. "Okay," said Rose. "Nothing dramatic, but we found a couple of things. What about you?"

"It might be nothing," replied Hal. He typed rapidly on his keyboard. Rose sat down. She could hear the electric hum of the room again, or rather feel it. Her mother blamed electromagnetism for everything from migraines to cancer. "You're taking years off your life, working in a building like that," she would say. "You need an outdoor job, something healthy. Like your sister - taking care of children, baking at home, real food, natural light, fresh air…"

"We found a record in the kitchen," said Sophie. She was looking at Butland. "Did you see it when you were there?"

"What?"

"A seven inch vinyl record, just on the side in the kitchen. A Rolling Stones record."

Butland laughed. "And?"

"It's worth about thirteen thousand pounds."

"What?"

"It's incredibly rare. There was a thirteen thousand pound record in a cardboard sleeve left out in the kitchen. Seems a bit odd, don't you think?"

Butland pulled a face. "He was probably just showing it to his guests."

"Maybe," said Sophie. "We sent it for fingerprinting."

Rose was looking at Hal. "So what have you got?"

Hal brought up some text on his screen. "Medical records," he said. "I've been looking at Carl Lane's medical records. You know we were wondering whether he and Georgia had a violent relationship? Well, I started to dig around, and it seems that Carl was no stranger to A&E."

Rose and Sophie leaned in closer to see his screen.

"February this year," he said. "Suspected broken wrist, bruising to his arm and face. He said he slipped over in the snow. His wrist was x-rayed but they decided it was just sprained."

"Okay," said Rose.

"Last Christmas. Boxing Day, the day of domestic arguments. He attended A&E in the evening with a head injury. He'd been drinking, he said, and he'd fallen over. No skull fracture but stitches in his scalp."

Rose nodded.

"Last summer… another fall. He said he came off a skateboard. Bruising to his hand and arm, no fracture." Hal scrolled down. "Going back to the previous year, he actually did have a fracture - broken finger. Again, injury to his arm and face - bruising to the side of his head, cut to his ear. He said he came off a friend's motorbike."

"He's accident prone," said Sophie.

"We should get more detailed statements from neighbours," said Hal. "We should ask specifically about accidents and injuries, and arguments, raised voices, fights."

Rose nodded. "People don't tend to think of men as victims of domestic violence so it's possible that it just hasn't occurred to anyone - we need to ask specific questions."

"It's still a big step to stabbing him," said Sophie.

There was a pause as they all sat thinking. It was impossible to know what went on behind closed doors. It was impossible to know what went on in people's minds. It was frustrating.

"We found a mark on the wall at the top of the stairs," Rose said. "It looked like someone had thrown a glass."

Hal nodded. "This is definitely a line of enquiry worth pursuing," he said.

"Yes, it is," said Rose. She wondered if she was being paranoid; was Hal behaving as if he was in charge? She sat straighter in her seat.

Hal tapped again at his keyboard, and Carl Lane's Facebook page appeared on the screen: a picture of Carl, stylishly dressed and laughing, standing in front of the Empire State Building. "He went to New York last September," Hal said. "Record hunting, meeting people, moving and shaking... a business-is-pleasure kind of trip. Georgia didn't go with him. I've looked back through her Facebook posts and she didn't mention him being gone at all. She didn't share any of his posts. Maybe she wasn't happy about the trip."

"Maybe." Rose could feel the headachy feeling creeping over her, as it always did in this office: a slow, dead feeling pressing on her skull. It was probably psychological. Her mother had horror stories about working nights, too: "The World Health Organisation has classified night work as carcinogenic," she told Rose. "It can cause diabetes, heart attacks, depression… it messes up your appetite and causes obesity." Rose thought about Nick, down at the custody desk, and his comforting biscuits.

"Okay," she said. "I guess we need to interview Georgia again."

Act Four

Interrogations

1

Nick couldn't stop thinking about Lucy. *This is it*, a voice in his head was saying, *this is where the sky falls in;* and there was something about the voice that suggested that something like this was bound to happen one day, and Nick had been a fool to think that he could make it through life safely just by being careful and methodical.

She would probably be fine. She was probably just stomping around, feeling angry and sorry for herself. *Teenagers do this all the time*. But what if she bumped into someone drunk, someone high, someone strange - or a gang of boys? Or what if she was reckless in her angry state, walking along the edge of the canal or crossing the dual carriageway? What if she got lost and panicked, and… he wasn't sure exactly what he was afraid of, but it felt as if the night could swallow Lucy up in some unnameable way. She wasn't a streetwise teenager, she wasn't one of those kids who washed up at the custody desk, all attitude and lies, who knew what ecstasy looked like and had sex with people they barely knew in strange bedrooms. Nick had seen in PC Lasky's eyes the assumption that he was a naive father, insisting against all evidence on the innocence of his little princess, but Nick knew that his kids really were from the young, quiet, 'late developer' mould. Ellie always knew where they were, they were never out past nine and their friends' parents usually drove them home. Lucy and her friend Alysha wanted to be fashion designers, and they spent their evenings in each other's bedrooms filling sketch pads with stylised drawings of sweeping gowns and angular jackets on hourglass figures. They ate sweet 'n' salty popcorn and ice lollies that turned their tongues orange. They got embarrassed and giggly when they talked about boys.

Lucy had never stormed off into the night before, so this was an event utterly without precedent; anything could happen. It was a leap into the unknown, off the edge of the world. Nick's only reference point was a memory from his own childhood, although he would have been younger than Lucy - nine, ten? - when after a row with his mother he decided to run away from home, and set off with a satchel full of random things and all the money he had been saving up for a Micro Machines playset. He walked and walked, powered by anger, until he was in a part of town so unfamiliar it may as well have been another country. It was daytime, but some boys his own age hanging around a sweet shop intimidated him with staring and posturing, so he ran, and became lost and out of breath, and close to tears. Drowning in self-pity he fantasised about how sorry his parents would be if he never came home, how vindicated he would be if he died and they regretted forever being mean to him, how they would weep at his funeral and blame themselves… and when he came to a high bridge over a dark river he stopped to consider tipping himself over the barrier. He could still remember, now, the shocking power of the emotions he felt, as he pressed his stomach hard against the metal barrier and leant over to look at the thick water, while anonymous, sightless cars whooshed past on the road behind him. It was a flood of youthful, uncontrollable emotions, violent and epic and intoxicating, which made him feel as huge and important as it was possible for a human to be: life and death and love and hate swirled around him, and it felt as if that moment had always existed and always would exist. It was a kind of immortality; the only kind of immortality. Somehow, he talked himself down... or maybe the flood simply passed and the emotions receded. He couldn't, now, remember the anti-climax; he couldn't remember why he decided not to jump, or even how he got home. He just knew that he was very, very close to being swept over that barrier by all that anger of youth, and he wondered, now, if Lucy could be tipped too far, as adolescents sometimes are, as even adults sometimes are, by the conspiracy of events and feelings that suddenly make suicide seem not only reasonable but mandatory. And with that thought came the thought that it was Nick's fault, that he had failed as a parent, that his daughter hated him so much that she would destroy herself to spite him.

With these thoughts marauding through his mind, he was trying to work.

He was reading out TWOC charges to four teenage boys, one by one, handing them the right forms, giving them a Youth Court date from the computer, handing them back their property and getting signatures, while the mother of the two Lewis boys continued to argue with him, her voice and face coming at him like physical blows he had to fend off. At least he had four fewer bodies to worry about in his cells - there was a moment of relief when they had all finally left the building, a sense of a job ticked off a list. But then there was Alan Stamper to think about, and he was more complicated.

Nick dialled the number on the piece of paper. As a faraway phone rang, he felt he was reaching into the unknown.

"Hello?"

"Hello? Is that Dave Stamper?"

"Yes, speaking." Could he trust this person?

"This is Sergeant Toft here, from the police station; I'm ringing about your brother Alan, who I have here in custody."

"Yeah, sure." The voice was eager to please.

"I understand you spoke to Alan earlier?" Nick had allowed Alan to ring his brother to explain the situation.

"Yeah, that's right, he told me he'd been arrested for hitting Carole and he asked if he could come and stay with me. That's no problem for me at all, I'm happy to have him, keep him away from Carole and all that."

"I am considering bailing him to your address, but I need to ask you a few questions…"

"Oh, absolutely; he'll be fine here, well away from her, here in Raynall. I could take him to work with me: I do shop fitting and they're always looking for an extra labourer - it would keep him out of trouble. I'd like to help him out, you know, straighten him out - my wife feels the same." He laughed. "I mean, he's getting a bit old for all that lairy fighting stuff now, isn't he? I'm not surprised Carole's had enough of him. It'd be good for him to come and stay with us for a bit, straighten him out. We don't drink."

"Would you be able to come and pick him up?"

"Absolutely."

"My concern would be that he'd try to come back here tomorrow and contact Carole…"

"Oh, don't worry, I won't let him do that."

Nick was pondering. He felt like a spinning coin, balanced but feverishly moving, not sure yet whether to fall heads or tails. Some bail decisions were hard, no matter how many thousands he had made. He didn't want to be taken for a fool, but neither did he want to go through life trusting no-one. The decision whether to grant bail was in some sense a weighing of a soul: did he see this person as inherently bad, inevitably destined to breach their bail and undeserving of pity, or did he see them as capable of good, as weak and fallible as any human but capable of nobility if given a chance?

As he was pondering Alan's situation, PC Whealdon came in to charge Jerome and Alice with going equipped and burglary of a shed. PC Whealdon hated paperwork and institutional computers, and Nick had to walk him through printing out the charge sheets. More bail decisions had to be made. Jerome had been in trouble before, but not for the last six months, and remarkably he had no history of failing to attend court; he also had a stable address with his mother. Alice was a different matter. Not only was her address vague - when she was booked in she described it as belonging to a friend she was staying with - but she was also already on bail for two shoplifting offences. Nick decided to remand her in custody, and booked a court hearing for the morning.

"Bring her out for charge first," he said.

Katrina brought Alice from her cell, again holding the frail elbow. Alice was agitated by the time she reached the desk. "Please, Serge," she began straight away, "don't lock me up, I can't do it again, I can't go back to Ripley Hall."

"You'll only be in the cell here tonight," said Nick. "Court tomorrow."

"But the court won't bail me if you don't!" Alice cried. "It never works like that!"

"You'll have a solicitor in the morning to make a bail application to the magistrates…"

"They'll say no!"

"You shouldn't have been out thieving," put in PC Whealdon.

Alice was big-eyed, looking up at Nick. "Give me a curfew," she said. "You can bail me with a curfew. I'll stay in six till six."

Nick was shaking his head. "I'm remanding you in custody on the grounds that you have committed offences whilst on bail…"

Alice started crying, alternately shouting and begging, and it suddenly felt to Nick that his whole life was a hailstorm of other people's traumas. He wanted to escape, right now; he needed shelter. He held himself together and recited procedural phrases to Alice without looking at her, handed the paperwork to PC Whealdon and stepped back from the desk with his jaw clenched and grim. "I have other people to deal with now," he said. "Katrina, could you help this officer deal with Alice."

He needed to breathe.

He yearned for a cigarette break, but the telephone was ringing and Aaron had disappeared.

"Custody."

"Hi, is this Nick Toft?"

"Yes."

"Oh hi, this is Jeb Kravitz. Pete Lasky asked me and Riz to look out for your daughter."

"Oh."

"We've been all around the area of the high school and into the park - we found a bunch of lads drinking cider in the park and moved them on, but they didn't have any girls with them."

Nick was trying to picture PC Kravitz as he spoke; he knew him only vaguely. Young, a bit cocky. "We were wondering where else we should look - I mean, maybe in the town centre, you know? Could she be round the back of the station?"

The back of the station was what older officers referred to as the red light district. Nick was simultaneously angry and scared. "No," he said, "she won't be there. But she might have walked towards town... keep looking. She's really young, she's just a kid."

"Yeah," said Jeb Kravitz. "She's fourteen, isn't she?"

"Yes, but a young fourteen. Small."

"Okay, we'll keep looking. Do you want us to call it in and get everyone looking?"

"No." Nick took a breath. "Not yet."

"Okay."

Not yet. He realised he was keeping his panic at bay by imposing different levels on the crisis. First step, ring around her friends and get a bobby or two out looking for her discreetly. If she's not found after - what? An hour? Two hours? - second step, report her as officially missing. Third step?

PC Whealdon had brought Jerome up to the desk to be charged. He was looking jittery and pink eyed. Nick tried to get a grip on himself.

"Right then," he said. "You court date is first thing in the morning, Jerome, because your co-accused is being refused bail."

"Yeah?" said Jerome. "Poor Ali. She'll be sweating it; she hates being locked up."

Nick found the plastic bag of Jerome's possessions that he had sealed up earlier and ripped it open. He pushed the contents across the desk.

"She pretends she's tough, but she's not you know." Jerome started shoving his phone and keys into the tight pockets of his tight jeans. "Her mum died of an overdose when she was fifteen. I try to look out for her…" He shrugged.

"You shouldn't have taken her out thieving then," said PC Whealdon.

"I told you, I didn't!"

"Sign here," said Nick.

The back door buzzed, and Nick squinted at the monitor. PC Lasky. Nick felt a sense of betrayal. How many other people had PC Lasky told about his daughter? Were all the uniformed officers on shift gossiping about him now?

He let PC Lasky in and Jerome out. PC Whealdon scowled one last time at the paperwork and went off upstairs. PC Lasky came up to the desk.

"Have you made a decision on Alan, Serge? I want to get him charged."

Nick was still a spinning coin. "I spoke to his brother. Do you know anything about him?"

"Never heard of him," said PC Lasky. "That's probably a good sign."

The back door buzzed again, and Nick looked at the monitor. "Who's that?" he mumbled, half to himself. There was an oldish man in a suit with a briefcase and bushy hair. Nick buzzed him in.

"I had a call from PC Kravitz," he said to PC Lasky. "He said you'd asked…"

"Oh yeah, I asked Jeb and Riz to have a look for your wayward daughter. They were just cruising around doing nothing, and they're young - they're pretty good at knowing what the kids get up to these days."

The oldish man in the suit came striding in from the corridor and put his briefcase up on the desk, flat, and looked over it at Nick. He was short, with bushy ginger hair and bushy ginger eyebrows. "Sergeant," he said. "I'm Philip Paley. Solicitor for Georgia Lane."

Nick nodded. "I'm just dealing with another case here…"

"I had a call from CID. They said they wish to interview my client yet again," said Mr Paley. He was using a forthright, clipped tone. "I want to make representations and I want to look at the custody record."

Nick nodded again. It was at times like this when his careful note taking was vindicated: he knew this officious gentleman would find nothing out of order. Or would he? Mistakes were always possible, weren't they? Nick had lost confidence in everything, tonight; he felt embattled, under siege. Right now he just wanted a cigarette in the fresh air, alone. "Of course," he said to Mr Paley. "If you'll just give me a moment." He turned back to PC Lasky. "Go on, we'll give Alan a chance," he said. "Bail with conditions" - he counted them off on his fingers - "one, residence at his brother's; two, not to go within two miles of his wife's address; three, not to attempt to contact her by phone, social media et cetera; and four, attending at Raynall Police Station every day at ten, two and six… no, scrap that, his brother's taking him to work. Let's just make it evenings, signing at the police station there every day at seven pm."

PC Lasky was nodding, and Nick felt decisive and - however briefly - back in control. "Now then," he said. "Mr Paley. What can I do for you?"

2

"I just want to make it clear," began Georgia's new solicitor, at the start of the recorded interview, "that my client has already been questioned twice, and she has co-operated fully and answered all questions, so unless you have any new evidence to put to her I'm advising her to say nothing more."

Rose nodded. Mr Paley was an irritating man, with his suit and his declaratory way of speaking and his briefcase which he liked to open and close with a flourish, but his announcement was not unreasonable and Rose was aware of the video camera in the corner of the room, effectively the eyes and ears of a jury. She adopted her own most patient and reasonable tone. "I understand," she said, gently, "but we do in fact have new evidence to put to Mrs Lane. That's why we need to ask her some more questions."

Hal had laid his own tablet computer down on the table in front of him and he was ready to read out the list of hospital admissions. He interlaced his fingers patiently. Rose, though, was going first. She looked at Georgia. "We had a good look around your kitchen," she began, "and we found something rather odd. Do you have any idea what that might be?"

It was good to start with an open question. It was a trick really: the suspect might think the police had found something they hadn't and start babbling. Here, though, Georgia just looked blank, completely blank - even empty. She seemed to have drifted out of herself since she had been given the sedative.

"Stop talking in riddles," said Mr Paley.

Rose nodded. "Okay. I'll explain. We found a seven inch record, a vinyl record, in its sleeve - 'Street Fighting Man' by the Rolling Stones."

Mr Paley snorted. "The relevance of this is…?"

"The relevance is that it's a very rare record, presumably at your house because of Carl's business. And when I say it's rare I mean it's valuable, very valuable, worth about thirteen thousand pounds. It's a very valuable item that must have been very precious to Carl, yet it was left out in the kitchen, where it could easily be damaged. It has a cardboard sleeve. Now, it seems to me that Carl must have brought it into the kitchen for a reason, perhaps to sell it to someone, or perhaps because he'd just bought it… so I'm asking you: did anyone else visit your house that day?"

"No," said Georgia.

"Had Carl been out to buy that record?"

"No."

"Why was it in the kitchen?"

"I don't know."

"Have you seen it?"

Georgia's face was expressionless. "Yes, I know the one you mean. It is valuable - Carl bought it a few weeks back… I don't know when." She sighed. "I don't know why he got it out. It doesn't matter. Maybe he was showing it to Jack and Annette." She shrugged. "Maybe they were trying to steal it."

"Steal it?"

"Maybe. Maybe they got hold of it and Carl was trying to get it off them, maybe that's why they killed him."

Rose paused. "You told me earlier that you were all in the garden."

"Yes."

"So Jack and Annette didn't go upstairs to Carl's room, did they?"

Georgia shrugged.

"Did they?"

"Maybe he brought it down to show them."

"And they tried to snatch it?"

Georgia shrugged again.

"You told us before that when you were upstairs you didn't hear any kind of argument or commotion in the kitchen."

Georgia shrugged and looked at her hands. She was no longer wearing a blanket over her shoulders, and the white paper suit was like a mask, as much a disguise as her Facebook profile. She was unreachable.

"This doesn't seem to me to be evidence," said Mr Paley. "Not against my client anyway. Perhaps it's Mr and Mrs McAllister who should be answering these questions."

Rose nodded, watching Georgia. She was completely blank, as blank as the shapeless white suit she wore. Her hands lay on the table in front of her, adorned with rings and shiny nails but completely still.

"So when you came into the kitchen, and Carl had been stabbed," said Rose, carefully, "where was this record?"

Georgia shrugged. "I have no idea. I didn't see it. I didn't even know it was there."

"What was being said, when you came into the room?"

"Nothing." Georgia's mouth twitched. "They didn't say anything. They were monsters. Carl was on the floor and his... they were fussing about with a tea towel, like he'd just had an accident or something."

There was a pause. Georgia hadn't looked up from her hands while she was speaking. Mr Paley clicked his pen impatiently. He was scribbling occasional illegible notes, his pen scoring the paper aggressively. Rose looked at Hal. "We have something else to ask you about," she said.

Hal came to life.

"Georgia," he said. "I've obtained Carl's medical records, and there are matters here that are causing me a lot of concern."

Georgia looked up at him.

"It appears that Carl was regularly turning up at A&E with unexplained injuries."

Georgia continued to look at him.

"It seems to me that he was suffering physical injuries far more frequently than is normal, which makes me wonder if something was going on at home."

He looked across and met Georgia's eyes.

"What are you talking about?" said Mr Paley irritably.

"So, for example, in February he went into A&E with bruising to his arm and face. Can you tell me about that?"

Georgia hesitated, staring at Hal. "He fell over on the ice. It was icy in February."

"Where did he fall?"

"In our driveway. Getting out of the car."

"What's your point?" said Mr Paley.

Hal ignored him. "Did anyone see him fall?"

Georgia shrugged. "No. I don't know. Maybe."

"Are you sure that he fell? You see, on Boxing Day, just a month or two earlier, he was in A&E with a head injury. Something had hit him on the head - there was a lot of blood, by all accounts, and he had to have stitches."

"Are you trying to say that she beat her husband?" asked Mr Paley, incredulously.

Hal shifted his gaze to look at him. "That's exactly what I'm saying, yes."

Georgia let out a cry. "You people!" She had come to life, now, and she was angry. "He fell over, okay? He was pissed, it was Christmas, he fell over and hit his head on a corner of the kitchen table. I didn't hit him."

"Were there any witnesses?"

"No! Shit…"

"Last summer he was in A&E with bruising to his hand and arm - and he had a broken finger before that."

"That was years ago! He broke his finger when he came off the back of Toby's motorbike. I wasn't even there. You can ask Toby about that, they were messing about off-road - shit, you people are unreal."

"So what happened last summer?"

"What?"

"When he had bruising to his hand and arm?"

"I don't know!"

"This is ridiculous," said Mr Paley.

"These are just the hospital admissions, Georgia," said Hal. "There could have been any number of incidents when he had injuries that weren't serious enough to need treatment."

"Do you have any evidence?" snapped Mr Paley.

"Something happened in your house at the top of the stairs," Rose chipped in. "There's a mark on the wall where it looks like something was thrown, like a drink."

Georgia stared at her.

"It looks quite recent."

Georgia started shaking her head in fury. "Yes, okay, yes... I threw a bottle of water. I remember, yes, we had an argument - everyone has arguments! Are you married?"

"What happened?" asked Rose.

"I threw a bottle of water, a plastic sports bottle - and no, I didn't throw it at *him*, I just threw it at the wall because I was mad, and it soaked the wall. I never threw anything at Carl, and I never hit him... you people - you people are unbelievable."

"Have you ever thrown anything else?"

"No!"

Georgia glared at Rose. Rose felt horrible. This was a horrible job. Either Georgia was a horrible liar, or Rose and Hal were horrible bullies.

"My *husband* is *dead* and you're trying to make me remember *arguments*." There were tears in Georgia's eyes. "I can't believe this."

"No, I can't believe it either," said Mr Paley. "This is all nonsense."

"This is a murder investigation," said Hal.

"So investigate," retorted Mr Paley. "Do your job properly - find some actual evidence instead of all this unfounded insinuation."

"Okay, okay," said Rose. "Let's all calm down. We'll end the interview there."

3

Nick had his packet of cigarettes cupped in his hand, but it seemed that every time he tried to head for the cool darkness outside the back door he snagged on something. He charged and bailed Alan Stamper, who was profusely grateful at being released, and kept repeating "I won't go near her, boss, you got my word on that" while he waited, twitching, for his brother to pick him up. PC Lasky rolled his eyes and disappeared before Nick could ask him again to look for Lucy. Every time the phone rang Nick's heart lurched, expecting news - good or terrible - about his daughter, but every time it was some trivial question or technical difficulty or message for someone else. Nick was dealing with fiddling work stuff while a real, heart-stopping crisis played out in his own life.

He found himself making deals with the universe. *If she comes home safe I'll...* what? Never take life for granted again? Do more with the kids? Be nicer to Ellie? He knew, though, that Lucy's continued disappearance wasn't really a punishment, or a trial, but rather a random, meaningless act of an unconscious universe. Anything could happen. He thought about fate, and his conversation with Joe. Of course, sometimes you could take your life in your hands and make choices and decisions, but sometimes - most of the time - you couldn't control anything, but were carried along, helplessly, by the world.

He wished he could see into the future and know how this would turn out. Lucy's disappearance might be nothing or everything. She might simply come home, unharmed, and go to bed, and after a burst of relief life would carry on as if nothing had happened; or she might not come home, and life might never be the same again. There was some moment in the future when Nick would either be back to normal, or devastated. Right now he was in limbo, just waiting to see which of his divergent futures was the real one. He had no way of knowing - he could only hang here, in this moment, right now.

Didn't Shakespeare write something about humans being the playthings of the gods?

Rose had come out of her interview with Georgia Lane, and she came up to Nick's desk and rested on her elbows.

"Is Georgia to go back to her cell?" Nick asked, looking round for Katrina.

Rose pulled a face. "Not yet. Mr Paley wants some time for a conference with his client."

Nick nodded. "He seems the type to throw spanners in the works."

"Whole toolboxes," said Rose. She saw the cigarettes in his hand. "Could I be cheeky and cadge another one of those?"

Nick had intended to be alone. "Uh, okay…"

"Not if you…"

"No, it's okay."

"Are you sure?"

"Absolutely. Let's go now, it looks like a relatively quiet moment. As quiet as it gets."

Outside, the night had not changed. Presumably the moon and stars had moved, but the car park, in its dome of light, was still and tranquil. Rose took the offered cigarette and Nick lit it for her.

" 'Receive what cheer you may'," she said, " 'the night is long that never finds the day'."

He looked at her.

She laughed. "It's from *Macbeth*. I googled it - I don't usually go around quoting Shakespeare from memory. It just seemed appropriate. This isn't one of my best nights."

"No breakthroughs?"

"No. No confessions, no witnesses, no devastating forensic, no smoking gun... and now the delightful Mr Paley to add to the mix." She was smiling, though. "The only thing I remember from *Macbeth* is 'Hubble bubble toil and trouble...' - is that it? The witches."

"It's 'Double, double, toil and trouble, fire burn and cauldron bubble'."

"That's it! It's a spell, isn't it? It's like a mantra, it gets stuck in your head."

Nick nodded, and blew out smoke.

"Are you okay?" asked Rose, looking at him closely.

"Yeah. No." He couldn't hide the anxiety that was saturating him. "Actually things have turned a bit stressful. I had a call from my ex wife. My fourteen year old daughter has stormed off out and no-one knows where she is."

Rose looked at him. *Please*, he thought, *don't say 'that's just what teenagers do'*. He knew that Rose didn't have children, and couldn't possibly imagine... He remembered Ellie had said to him once, years ago: "You're never really gone from my life, you know. I look at the kids, and I see you - Lucy's got your stubbornness, and Jo has your infuriating way of doing everything slowly and in order." At the time he had heard only the criticism, but he saw now that it was true that he and Ellie would always be connected by their children. They would never get back together - as a married couple, they didn't work - but they were connected by the past and the future: their offspring. And right now, at this moment, they were directly connected by their common worry: he could almost feel Ellie, out there in another part of town, transmitting her anxiety as he transmitted his.

"That must be an awful worry," Rose said. "Especially when you're stuck at work, waiting for news."

Nick nodded, helplessly.

"Has she done this before?"

"No, never. She's not that kind of kid."

"She'll probably be okay. She'll just walk about feeling angry and then go home."

"Yeah."

"It's the kids that take drugs and know the wrong kind of people that are in danger."

"That's true."

"It's a pretty safe town actually. Not exactly the big bad city."

Nick smiled. At that moment, the night was silent - there wasn't even the sound of traffic. "You're absolutely right," he said. "She'll probably be fine." He dropped flecks of ash. "I just… it's just horrible not knowing where she is."

Rose nodded sympathetically. She moved forward and gently touched his arm, then moved away, a little embarrassed. "I'm sure she'll be fine."

Nick nodded again, emphatically, and took a drag on his cigarette. "She will. Most likely she'll be fine." He breathed out. "It's just part of having kids, isn't it? You're better off without them."

Rose smiled and looked at the ground.

"I mean, sorry, I shouldn't have said that," amended Nick. "You might have wanted them and… it's none of my business, sorry."

"No, it's okay," said Rose.

There was a pause while neither of them said anything, but just smoked, and Rose looked thoughtfully at her shoes. "I kind of chose not to have kids. When Gavin and I first got married, we were young and ambitious and we agreed that we never wanted children… but I guess that if our relationship had worked out we might have changed our minds. That's what all my friends did. All of them started out in their twenties not wanting to be tied down by children, wanting careers and romantic holidays and all that, but all of then hit their thirties and turned broody… and then they all left me for the world of toddler groups and Disney." She laughed. "They were always visiting petting zoos and water parks. The only pubs they'd go to were the ones with those manic cages full of plastic balls."

Nick laughed.

"So I lost all my friends to parenthood," she went on, "but Gavin and I never did change our minds. And our marriage got more and more difficult… sorry, I'm talking about myself."

"That's okay. I need to take my mind off Lucy. I'm not doing any good fretting about her."

"I'm sure she'll be fine." Right now, the world seemed so peaceful that Nick could almost believe that she would be fine, that Lucy was just out in the cool night air, calming down, looking at the stars and feeling better and deciding to go home.

But what if she was lost? She didn't have her phone. What would she do?

Rose stubbed out her cigarette. "I guess we should get back to work," she said. "Will you be okay?"

"Yep, I'm fine." Nick nodded. He was talking to himself as well as to Rose. "Lucy will be okay - she's just having an adventure."

Rose smiled. "That's it," she agreed. "She's just having an adventure."

4

Trudging alone up the stairwell towards the CID office, Rose wondered whether she regretted not having children. It was an impossible question, really. Her life would have been different, of course, but there are so many ways in which life can be different, and we can only imagine the other paths we might have taken, never experience them. Would her life have been more stressful? Emotionally richer? More complicated? More fulfilling? It was impossible to know, and meaningless to ask.

She reflected that it was a feature of middle age to look back over life and wonder how you got here. Decisions were made, but there was so much chance and happenstance that nothing about the path was truly chosen; Rose had never had much of a plan anyway. She had met Gavin and fallen in love; she had fallen in step with him, with nothing more than the vague assumption that they would walk together for a time. She had joined the police force because it seemed to be a decisive move - a definite career rather than something woolly in "retail management" or "product development" - looking back at her student self, she realised that she wanted career decisions to be made for her, and so she chose a broad, straight path, paved with concrete and signposted. It felt safe. She never actually pictured herself beyond the first year, and she realised, now, that it was not in her nature to plan into the future. Perhaps that was wise: she was simply giving herself up to the tides and currents of the world rather than pretending she could swim against them.

She reached the top of the empty, echoing stairwell and pushed through the double doors into the empty, echoing corridor. One of the fluorescent lights was flickering, a barely perceptible twitch. Rose pushed through the door of the CID office and was aware of movement in response to her entrance, as if she was a teacher entering a classroom. Hal jumped up from where he had been sitting, his legs long and eager as a grasshopper's, while Sophie swung her chair around to greet Rose.

"There you are!" called Hal. "We wondered where you'd got to."

"Why, what's happened?"

"Carl Lane's parents. I've tracked them down - they've just got home from the hospital. They were at his bedside. They live in Chardly." Chardly was a village just outside town. Hal was already fingering his car keys. "I thought Sophie and I might go out and talk to them… we can express sympathy and all that but also see whether they have anything to say about Carl and Georgia's relationship, whether it occurred to them that Carl might be in danger. What do you think?"

Rose nodded. "Yes, it's a good idea to get their take on it."

Sophie stood up. "You don't want to speak to them yourself?"

Rose shook her head. "No, you two go."

Hal and Sophie swept out. Butland was drumming on his desk, making ripples in his coffee. His computer was on and he appeared to be tidying up some paperwork on another case. Rose sat down, just as the phone rang. Ehlen answered it and passed it to her.

"It's the DCI again," he said. Butland looked up.

"Oh." Rose took the receiver, and looked at her own reflection in the dark screen of her computer. "Olding here."

"Rose, listen, I've been told there's a lot of media interest in this murder case."

Rose said nothing. It was hard to picture a clamouring media: the CID office was silent and soporific, closed off behind its metal blinds, and outside in the night it had felt as if the whole world was asleep. She realised now that there was a gathering storm of phone calls and emails happening somewhere, and the morning was approaching like a hurricane.

"So I'm going to have to make some sort of statement, first thing," the DCI went on. "I've told them to fix a press conference for eight-thirty - it's a nice, efficient time, makes us sound on top of things. It's looking like TV cameras will be there." Did he sound nervous? She didn't think so. He was so smooth and professional. Could Rose ever do his job? Did she want to? "So I'll need you to brief me fully at seven. And I will need to have something to tell them. Not just an appeal for information - I don't want to look like we've got nothing."

"No, of course," said Rose.

"So I'll see you at seven then."

"Seven."

He was gone.

Rose handed the dead receiver back to Ehlen and avoided Butland's questioning eyebrows. She flicked on her computer so that she had something to look at. She knew that Sophie thought she was giving ground to Hal by letting him be the one to interview the victim's parents, but Rose wasn't sure that racing out into the night again was the best way to deal with this case, or the best was to signal her authority; she was, after all, the Inspector on this team, the conductor rather than the lead violin. It was time for her to sit in the office and do some thinking.

It was difficult to think, though, under such a low ceiling. She rested her eyes on the screen in front of her, without seeing. This case was getting nowhere. Everything was so weak and inconsequential: they were scratching around for scraps. Sometimes work was like that - sometimes it went well, sometimes it didn't; sometimes you got lucky, sometimes you got nowhere. Of course, when it went well that reflected well on your abilities, and when it didn't there was always someone ready to whisper that you weren't up to the job. Rose was looking at Carl's Facebook page again. Was there anything they'd missed? A clue staring her in the face? Posts about music, posts about trips; happy selfies - Carl had a way of holding his head, a look of studied cool - had he practised in the mirror? Probably. There was nothing about injuries, nothing about the Rolling Stones record. Nothing about Jack or Annette, or even Georgia; his Facebook page was an advert for his professional life. There was nothing useful here.

She was just looking at pictures of a dead man. He could tell her nothing.

There might be a whole story behind his death. Perhaps international record thieves, dressed in black, had broken into his house and lain in wait for him. Perhaps a rival vinyl dealer had come round in a fit of vengeful - but very quiet - fury. Perhaps he had fallen on the knife after all; there had been stranger deaths.

It seemed most likely that the simplest theory was the right one, and Georgia was capable of sudden, violent outbursts. Perhaps Hal would come back from Carl's parents waving a damning statement: perhaps they had had their suspicions all along, perhaps Carl had confided in them, perhaps they could recall occasions when he had been afraid of his wife and even wondered aloud whether one day she might kill him. The case would be solved. Of course, Hal would take credit for it… did that matter? Rose sighed. She didn't want to be petty.

She thought about Nick. He was down there in the basement, at the sharp end, and he was worrying about his child; his worries that night were life and death stuff, not petty workplace competition. She wished she knew exactly what to say to him to make him feel better. She wanted to be there for him, to be the one person who could help… she was falling in love, wasn't she? Silly. She took a breath and focussed on her computer.

Carl's medical records. She could just imagine a defence barrister pulling this evidence apart - it was so circumstantial and desperate. Carl was clearly an active, exciting kind of guy: falling over drunk and riding on friends' motorbikes were the kind of things he got up to. Scared of his wife? A jury would find that hard to believe. Rose needed evidence, proper evidence, but there was none. Maybe no-one would ever know what happened.

"Do you want a coffee?" Butland had sidled over. He probably wanted to know what the DCI had said.

"Yes, that'd be great, thanks." Rose flashed him a quick smile and then set her eyes on her screen. There was nothing useful here. And the clock at the top said 04:02.

5

It was 04:02. Nick was beginning to feel that everything was slipping away from him.

He looked at the whiteboard without seeing it. Had he updated the review times? There was no news about Lucy. Should he call more officers and ask them to look for her? Jeb and Riz were a pair of jokers, probably just cruising around, chatting, laughing, parking up to eat burgers... He forced himself to focus on the whiteboard. Brian Dunn - he'd been there for hours, he needed to be dealt with - and in cell seven, Luke Hall, who the hell was that? Oh yes, breach of bail, for court in the morning. Nick felt that his heart was racing - a frantic flutter at his throat like a fly beating itself mindlessly against a window - while his brain was moving slowly, wading through heavy water and fumbling to catch hold of the things that were swirling around him.

Brian Dunn. He rang the officer in the case, PC James.

"Do you want to come down here and charge Mr Dunn now?"

"I need to interview him first."

Nick had forgotten.

"Is he coherent enough to interview?" asked PC James.

Nick didn't know.

"Yes," he said, "just about. Make your way down here." He rang off.

He needed to concentrate on work. He took up an inky cloth and wiped Jerome's name off the board. He had already wiped Alan Stamper. Should he have released Alan? He wasn't so sure now. He had taken a risk. He should have called the Domestic Violence Unit. Did he check Alan's record? He couldn't remember. No, he hadn't checked Alan's record. What if Alan went straight round to his wife's and killed her?

The back door buzzed: another officer, with another prisoner. He let her in. Aaron was in the kitchen, drinking coffee. He was very deliberate about his breaks, standing still and looking at nothing, and he would turn a truculent expression towards Nick if he was even asked a question. Nick decided not to ask his opinion on Brian Dunn but instead let PC James find out what condition his suspect was in.

The phone rang. Nick jumped. His first though was about Alan Stamper turning up at his wife's with murderous intent; his second, almost simultaneous, thought was for Lucy. The two merged together in his mind and fear hit him like a punch.

"Hello?"

"Hi, is that the officer in charge of the cells?"

It was a journalist, young and amateurish and trying to sound important, wanting to know about the Lane murder.

"You know full well I can't give you any information." It was an opportunity for Nick to release some of his tension by raising his voice, and before he knew it he was almost shouting. Even Aaron looked round in surprise. "Goodbye."

It was unlike Nick to lose his temper, ever, especially at work. He looked up at the officer he had let in, PC Jen

Munro, who had left her suspect on the bench in the corridor and was looking at Nick with concern. "Tough night?" she asked.

"You could say that." Nick forced a smile. Jen Munro was always jolly: short-haired, stocky, capable, no-nonsense. "What have you got?"

"Shoplifting."

"Shoplifting? On a Sunday night?"

Jen laughed. "I know! Quite an achievement, eh? He was in a petrol station, stuffing chocolate bars in his pants, not even hiding it - he's off his face on something."

"Let's get him booked in." Routine - Nick needed to focus on routine. He tapped at the computer, business-like, and took control of himself. PC Munro brought in a glassy-eyed boy in an orange t-shirt, who seemed not quite certain of his own name and address but answered politely and gravely, as if he was trying his best to help. Nick calmed down as he went through his familiar procedures, reciting his lines and completing his forms, safe behind his high desk. His anxiety, though, remained, like a stone in his shoe or grit in his eye.

He was now suffering from memories of Lucy, little intense moments popping into his head like sharp thorns: memories of her as a small child, the movement of her hair, the feel of her hand in his, an image of her on a swing in the park, refusing to get down and jerking back and forth so that the chains rattled, wailing for one more push. He remembered, painfully, the sensation of frustration and love as he gave in and she wriggled with pleasure. Almost at once he was pricked by another image: her thirteenth birthday, when he dropped by with her present and she was painting her fingernails in different colours; he could smell the nail polish and see her hair drooping over her forehead as she concentrated. Another memory - there was no order to these jagged scraps of the past - Lucy was just a week old, tiny in an enormous pram, still wrinkled as a wet tissue, emitting a quiet keening sound.

He had memories of Lucy from her very beginnings, her own amnesiac years: part of being a parent was carrying these memories for another person, the memories of who they were when they didn't know themselves. Perhaps that was why parents were so possessive of their children. Your children were never quite separate beings: there was a part of them that belonged to you, deeply embedded in you, that they themselves could never reach.

Nick could remember Lucy even before she was Lucy, when she was the new baby, inside Ellie, fragile and still not quite dependable, a possibility - a probability - but not yet a certainty. They had lived in a rented flat when Joe was born, the bedroom so small that the double bed was pressed against the wall and they had to climb over one another to get out, but they bought a house while Ellie was pregnant with Lucy, and when Lucy was a baby the family were still growing into the house, still discovering it and shaping it, painting the walls in bright colours and then worrying about the baby breathing the fumes. Parenthood was one new challenge after another - stair gates and potty training and nursery - and having gone through it with Joe didn't make it any easier with Lucy, Nick discovered, because children are all different: individuals, with their own eccentricities and passions. Lucy hated her cereal soggy, and ate it so fast she was nearly sick; she insisted on shoes with laces, instead of the velcro Joe loved, and she sat on the floor in the middle of the hall to tie them, infuriatingly slowly, her fingers tiny and nimble, tugging the laces taut and then carefully looping the bows, chanting instructions to herself as she did so. In bed she wore thick pyjamas, he remembered; even in midsummer she liked to sleep deep under the duvet with just her sweaty hair showing. Her remembered her toes sticking out from the baggy pyjama bottoms as she came downstairs in the morning; he remembered the way she plonked down each step, and the smell of her when he leaned down to kiss the top of her head before he rushed off to work.

The phone rang.

"Yes?"

"Is that the custody desk?"

"Yes."

"We've got someone up here at the enquiry desk asking about Alan Stamper."

"What about him?"

"It's..." the voice faded out, talking to someone in the background. "It's - yes, madam, please take a seat - it's his wife, she says she just wants to know where he is." There were a number of voices in the background, indignant and querulous.

"Tell her to contact PC Lasky," Nick said, firmly. At least he knew now she wasn't dead. "In fact, page him - he's probably somewhere in the building." He rang off and turned around. "Aaron? Can you put this young man in cell six?"

Aaron looked at him for a moment, then nodded and gulped the last of his coffee.

"I'll get back out there then," said PC Munro, with a grin, resting her hands on the baton and pepper spray that clung lumpily to her belt.

Nick took a breath. "Could I ask a favour?"

"Sure."

He leaned forward across the desk. Aaron was taking the docile shoplifter down the corridor. "My daughter's gone missing - she had a row with her mum and stormed off out - you know, teenage stuff, but she's not come home yet and I'm getting worried. Could you have a look around? She left the house on Bramwell Street, near the high school; she can't have got far."

"Of course." PC Munro looked serious.

"She's fourteen, small, long brown hair, wearing a green jacket, sort of camo green."

"She's on her own?"

"Yes."

"Could she have gone down the park? There were loads of kids down there earlier; something was going off."

"PC Kravitz said he moved on some boys who were drinking…"

"That was just the tail end of it. There was all sorts going on in the park, kids running feral - someone lit a fire in the woods. There were girls down there too. Someone said they were all swimming in the lake… midsummer madness. Have you checked the hospital?"

"Not yet."

"I'll look about for her, anyway." PC Munro was nodding and looking serious. "I'll let you know if I see or hear anything."

Nick was in a spin again. He hadn't even thought of ringing the hospital. He buzzed PC Munro out and picked up the phone, but PC James had appeared, striding in breezily. "Ready to interview Dunn."

"Aaron? Could you get Brian Dunn out?" Nick stood, holding the phone, waiting. Katrina came back from the cells and ticked the whiteboard to confirm she had checked on various prisoners, and then she squeezed past Nick and went into the kitchen. The phone in Nick's hand rang and he nearly dropped it.

"Hello?"

"Hi, it's the enquiry desk again, I can't raise PC Lasky. Look, this woman just wants to know if Alan Stamper's still here or if he's been bailed."

"He's been bailed. He's got a condition not to come near her. He's in Raynall."

"Thank you." The harassed voice rang off. Aaron appeared with Brian Dunn. He was wearing a paper suit with a blanket wrapped around him like a wizard's cloak.

"Right then, Brian," said PC James. "Ready to answer some questions?"

"Of course, officer," said Brian, and then threw up all over the floor.

Act Five

Confessions

1

Butland was laughing.

"I think PC Lohan's trying to make a point," he said. "You asked him for a more detailed statement and he's sent you a thesis."

Rose clicked on the email attachment to open the statement on her screen. It was certainly lengthy. PC Lohan was off duty now and she imagined him at home, furiously jabbing with two fingers at his own laptop, bitching to his sleepy wife about his unceasing job. "I just hope there's something useful in it," she said.

"I wouldn't hold my breath," snorted Butland.

Rose settled down in her uncomfortable chair to read the statement.

> On Sunday 27 May my partner PC SYMONS and I received a call to attend at 6 RIVERSIDE VIEW following a report of an assault. We were informed that an adult male was seriously injured and that an ambulance had been called. We arrived at the address at 15:38 and parked our vehicle in front of the house. As we disembarked I immediately saw a woman I now know to be GEORGIA LANE, DOB 13/02/89, a white female, long blond hair, slim, approximately 5'9", in the doorway of the house. The

front door was open. She was in a distressed and angry state, and she appeared to be heavily under the influence of alcohol. I also saw at once that there was what appeared to be blood on her hands.

Riverside View is a residential street and since this was a sunny Sunday afternoon there were a number of children playing on bicycles and scooters. Seeing us and Ms LANE, a number of children accumulated in the front garden. Adult neighbours also came out of their homes to ask what was happening. Ms LANE came down her driveway to shout angrily and abusively at her neighbours, accusing them of coming to "gawp". She was quite aggressive and threatening and I formed the opinion from her appearance and manner that she had consumed a considerable quantity of alcohol. I also saw that there was blood splattered on her top, which was a pale green colour and short sleeved.

Rose paused to think about the clothing that had been seized and bagged up for Forensics. The blood was Carl's, of course; that was all Forensics could say. Perhaps one day they would be able to examine the pattern of blood splashes and model accurately the flight of the droplets, like modelling the path of a bullet or rewinding a motorway pile up, to determine exactly what had happened; but for now, blood splashes just meant that a quantity of blood had been spilled and the wearer of the clothing was close by. It was interesting that Georgia had been so angry and abusive, and interesting, too, that PC Lohan had considered her to be drunk. Perhaps Rose had not given quite enough weight to just how much the occupants of 6 Riverside View had drunk that afternoon. Alcohol could make people behave irrationally and extravagantly. They could easily do things they would regret - or things they would not otherwise have the courage to do.

I left PC SYMONS to speak to Ms LANE and I proceeded into the house. I am unable to say whether any windows were open. My priority was to find the injured person. I went in through the front door and into the hallway, past a flight of stairs, to an open door, through which I could see into the kitchen, which was at the back of the house. I proceeded into the kitchen.

In the kitchen I encountered three persons. I now know them to be: CARL BRADLEY LANE, DOB 07/06/88, the injured person; JACK MCALLISTER, DOB 20/05/85 of 9 RIVERSIDE VIEW, white male, short brown hair and short brown beard, slim build, approximately 5' 10", wearing blue cargo shorts and a blue t-shirt; and ANNETTE

MCALLISTER, DOB 04/01/90 of 9 RIVERSIDE VIEW, white female, brown hair in a short bob, slim build, approximately 5'2", wearing a blue and yellow patterned summer dress.

CARL BRADLEY LANE was lying on the floor between the kitchen table and the fitted units. He was lying on his side, curled into a foetal position. He was wearing a dark t-shirt, blue shorts and beige flip flops. I could see blood pooling beneath his neck and matting his hair. He appeared to have a red and white gingham cloth wrapped around his throat. It was soaked with blood. Upon further inspection I saw the black handle and part of the blade of a large kitchen knife protruding from the left side of his neck, which was uppermost. I could not say how long the blade was because it was embedded in his neck. His eyes were wide open but glazed and he did not seem to see me. His mouth was also open and making a gurgling sound. I could not be sure whether he was trying to speak. His body was shaking.

JACK MCALLISTER was kneeling on the floor beside MR LANE. He had blood on his hands and clothing and he appeared to be attempting to assist and comfort MR LANE. He was repeating the words "You'll be alright mate" in a reassuring tone. ANNETTE

> MCALLISTER was standing up nearby. She too had blood on her hands and clothing, and a splash of blood on her chin. She looked at me when I entered and said "He's hurt, please help."

It was interesting, Rose thought, how calm the McAllisters appeared in comparison with Georgia. Too calm? Or simply responsible bystanders responding to a domestic assault?

> I knelt down beside MR LANE and saw immediately that he was seriously injured, with a potentially life threatening wound. I called in to the Control Room to say that the ambulance was urgently needed. At this point PC SYMONS followed me into the kitchen and since he has advanced first aid training I stood up to allow him to attend to MR LANE. MR MCALLISTER also stood up, and I asked him what had happened. At this point he shrugged his shoulders and shook his head. He appeared to be in a state of shock. I then turned to MRS MCALLISTER and asked her what had happened. She said: "I don't know. He fell on the knife."

He fell on the knife. It was Annette who first came up with that, not Georgia, and she said it right at the scene, in Jack's hearing, and in contradiction of the things she had said since. Rose chewed her lip and read on.

> At this point MS LANE returned to the house and entered the kitchen. She was now shouting abuse at MR and MRS MCALLISTER and accusing them of "stabbing" MR LANE. They both appeared to be shocked and intimidated. I attempted to calm MS LANE down. I put myself between her and MRS MCALLISTER and pointed out that her behaviour was not helping her husband. She continued to shout and gesticulate and I was concerned that she would attack MRS MCALLISTER.
>
> At this point the paramedics arrived. My priority was now to create a space for them to attend to the injured person, so I attempted to move MS LANE into the hallway. The front door was still open and I could see curious children outside, so I manoeuvred MS LANE into the living room. She continued to remonstrate with me hysterically and refused to sit down. PC SYMONS then came into the room with MR and MRS MCALLISTER.

At this point MRS MCALLISTER told me that MS LANE had stabbed MR LANE. I asked her if she had seen it happen and she said yes. MS LANE then turned on MRS MCALLISTER, calling her an evil liar, and I was concerned there would be a violent incident. I formed the opinion that there were sufficient grounds to arrest MS LANE on suspicion of MALICIOUS WOUNDING OR ASSAULT OCCASIONING GRIEVOUS BODILY HARM and so I accordingly arrested her.

I noted down the time of the arrest, which was 16:07, and her comment on arrest, which was "What I'm his wife why are you arresting me".

At this point PC BRIDGES and PC LIN arrived at the house and I asked them to remove MS LANE and convey her to the Central Police Station. They proceeded to do so. MS LANE continued to shout that it was "them" that stabbed MR LANE, "them" meaning MR and MRS MCALLISTER. I formed the opinion that in all the circumstances there were sufficient grounds to arrest ANNETTE MCALLISTER and JACK MCALLISTER on suspicion of MALICIOUS WOUNDING OR ASSAULT OCCASIONING GRIEVOUS BODILY HARM, so I proceeded to do so.

I noted down the time of ANNETTE MCALLISTER's arrest as 16:11, and her comment on arrest as "What are you talking about you must be kidding this is a domestic".

I noted down the time of JACK MCALLISTER's arrest as 16:14, and his comment on arrest was "I don't get this why are you taking me it was Georgie that stabbed him".

Rose drummed her fingers on the desk. Nothing was clear cut: it had been a confused picture right from the start. There were no witnesses, just one angry woman and two people obfuscating.

PC SYMONS and myself escorted MR and MRS MCALLISTER to our vehicle, and put them in the back. We then waited for the arrival of PS LEMMING and PC HARDY, who attended just as the ambulance was leaving with MR LANE. I conferred with PS LEMMING and she confirmed that she would take charge of the crime scene. PC SYMONS and myself then conveyed MR and MRS MCALLISTER to the Central Police Station.

While we were in the vehicle MRS MCALLISTER stated that she was pregnant, but MR MCALLISTER stated that she was not. I informed MRS MCALLISTER that if she was pregnant then she should notify the custody sergeant on arrival at the police station. MRS MCALLISTER then started to cry and stated that MS LANE had stabbed MR LANE but that she hadn't meant to. I formed the opinion that MRS MCALLISTER was heavily under the influence of alcohol.

MR MCALLISTER then stated that it might have been an accident. At first MRS MCALLISTER agreed with him but then she began to implicate MS LANE again, stating that it was a terrible tragedy and MS LANE would regret what she had done. At this point MRS MCALLISTER calmed down and asked if she would be able to get a cup of tea at the police station.

I informed her that the custody sergeant would deal with her request. We arrived at the Central Police Station and conveyed MR and MRS MCALLISTER into the custody area, where custody sergeant PS DAVID INGLETON proceeded to book them in. PC BRIDGES and PC LIN were seizing the clothing of all three suspects for forensic examination.

PC SYMONS and myself did not return to RIVERSIDE VIEW. By this time it was 17:05. I wrote my initial statement and forwarded it to CID, who were taking charge of the case.

Rose finished reading the statement and considered what to do next. It was definitely worth questioning Annette again. She wondered whether to wait until Hal got back, since he had been present for the other interviews. She could go ahead with Butland or Ehlen instead, but it would be a snub to Hal, and Hal might have useful input. She looked up. The room was peaceful except for the regular sound of Ehlen clicking his mouse as he gazed intently and inscrutably at his screen. Butland was picking his back teeth with his fingernail and watching something on his phone. She decided to wait for Hal.

2

The duty doctor had arrived to see Brian Dunn. It was a young woman this time this time, tousle-haired and a bit spotty, so young that Nick felt all the irreversible weight of his own age. The cleaner was still mopping the floor desultorily. After being sick again Brian had warbled: "I'm dreadfully sorry, I think I may have a touch of food poisoning" and Nick had decided it was safest to get a doctor in to him again.

As the doctor made notes from the custody record, Katrina came to stand at the desk and catch Nick's eye. He moved over to her.

"Stuart's not answering his phone," she said breathlessly.

Nick nodded. "Okay," he said. "Do you want to go?"

"Yes," she said. "Yes, I do."

Nick nodded again.

"What about the fifteen minute checks on Georgia Lane?" Katrina asked.

Nick thought quickly. "I'll get Aaron to do them." He nodded again. "You go."

He could try calling for cover, for someone to replace Katrina for the rest of the shift - but he knew there would be no-one available. It was 04:28, less than two hours to go before the shift finished at six. He just needed to hold things together until then.

What if Lucy wasn't found before then? It was unthinkable that dawn could come, that it could be morning, and Lucy could still be missing. The duty doctor was talking to him and he was just nodding, without hearing. His anxiety made him feel like a frightened animal, fight or flight chemicals rushing through his raw veins. It was difficult to concentrate.

"Aaron?"

Where had he gone?

"Aaron!"

The duty doctor gave him a sympathetic smile. Nick looked up and down the corridor. "I'll take you to him myself," he muttered to the doctor, and found his fingers were actually shaking slightly as he unlocked the door to Brian Dunn's cell.

The back door was emitting impatient buzzes; someone wanted to be let in. Dunn was sitting calmly in his cell, wrapped in his blanket, so Nick took the decision to leave the doctor there, with the cell door open, while he rushed back to the desk to look at the back door monitor. He nearly fell over the 'Wet Floor' sign that the cleaner had left. Incredibly, it was Aaron outside the back door.

Nick buzzed him in and called out: "Where did you go?"

Aaron came towards the desk looking surprised. "I just had to go out to my car to get something," he said.

Nick was nodding again, and trying to be calm, trying to behave normally. "Okay, look," he said. "Katrina had to go home - family emergency - so I need you to take over the fifteen minute checks on Georgia Lane, as well as the fifteen minute checks on Brian Dunn - are we still doing them?" He squinted at the hieroglyphics on the whiteboard. "We need to get a hold of this lot, we need to keep on top of things." The board was a confusion of names and numbers and squiggles. "When did we last check on Annette McAllister?"

Aaron looked blank.

"Okay, well, Katrina hasn't written it down, so I need you to go and check on her now. And keep an eye on Brian Dunn" - the phone had started ringing - "the doctor's in the cell with him, I left the door open, check she's okay." Nick picked up the phone. "Custody."

It was PC Lasky. "Someone's told Alan's wife he's at his brother's," he said. "It's all kicking off in Raynall."

"What?"

"His wife turned up there with some of her mates - a whole pack of them practically out to lynch him… there are Raynall officers attending but Alan's called me, so I think I'd better go over there, see if I can calm it all down before it turns into a riot. Thought I'd let you know."

"Okay."

PC Lasky rang off, and Nick stood there holding the phone.

He needed to get a proper grip on everything. He was making mistakes, and he was someone who didn't make mistakes. He needed to take control. He needed, first, to check in with Ellie. She was supposed to be ringing Lucy's friends, and she hadn't called to let him know whether she'd turned up any information. He desperately needed some good news.

He dialled Ellie's home number, the number that used to be his.

It rang - three times, four times. Five times. Six times. A click, and the answerphone kicked in. Why wasn't she sitting by the phone? Had she gone out looking for Lucy? He had Ellie's mobile number somewhere. Probably. He waited impatiently through the slow message and the long beep.

"Hi, it's me, Nick, are you there? Pick up."

Silence. There was something about speaking to an answerphone that made him feel as if he was looking into a deep, dark well. He spoke again into the void. "Are you there? Is there any news?"

To his relief, he heard a clicking sound, like a phone being handled clumsily, and then Ellie's voice, sleepy: "Nick?"

"Yes, it's me, any news?"

"Oh, Nick, yeah, she came home, thank God."

"She's home?"

"Yeah."

There was a pause as relief and anger crashed over Nick. "Jesus, Ellie, you could've rung me to tell me - I've been really worried. I've been sending half the bobbies in town out looking for her... shit."

"I'm sorry, I didn't think."

"I've been worried as hell, I've been thinking all sorts..."

"Okay, I said I'm sorry!" She raised her voice, meeting his anger with her own. "I've had more to think about than you."

"I'm her dad..."

"Oh you're her dad now, are you, you want to be involved now, do you? You think you have some kind of right to be involved in her life? You only see her on birthdays and Christmas, you've done nothing..."

"Hey..."

"... she's nothing to you, you've not raised her; just because Joe wants to come round to yours once doesn't mean you're suddenly a fucking great dad you know.

I've brought those kids up on my own - even when you were here you weren't really here."

"Hey…"

Aaron and the doctor had come back in, up to the desk, and were looking at Nick. He could feel himself red-faced and breathing fast. He turned away, like a hunted animal, and stepped into the tiny kitchen with his back to the world.

"This isn't fair…" he began.

"Fair! I lost relationships because I was a single mother. Christian left me because he didn't want to raise another man's children. Those kids are mine, I've done everything, I'm the one who brought them up; you were never around, even when you lived here. You can't just come sweeping in now they're grown up and everything's easy…"

"This is all about Joe coming round to mine, isn't it? You're punishing me because Joe wanted to come to me…"

"Oh you're such a great dad now, aren't you? Can't you see that Joe is just using you to get at me?"

"This is sick!" There was no door on the kitchen. Nick could sense that Aaron and the doctor were just seven or eight feet behind him, silent. He took a deep breath. He had never made a personal phone call at work before, let alone used the custody phone to have a private argument. "I have to go," he said, and cut her off. She was shouting something. He stood, breathing heavily, looking at the tiny sink in front of him and the peeling 'Wash Your Hands' sticker on the wall.

He turned around. Aaron looked away. The young doctor gave him a sympathetic smile. "Everything okay?" she asked.

"Yes," said Nick, coming over to the desk. "Yes, yes, actually, everything is fine." Lucy was home, she was safe; it was all over. He tried to calm down. "How's Mr Dunn?"

"I'm not sure, to be honest. His temperature's high, his signs are a bit odd, and I'd like to transfer him to hospital." She offered another sympathetic smile. "I'm guessing that will give you a headache."

Nick felt like he was coming up from being deep underwater.

"No... no, it's okay," he said. "I can just bail him to come back another day. He's only in for drunk in charge, it's not murder."

"That's great."

"I'd better just check his record." Nick turned to the computer. He typed in Brian's name, and looked at the doctor. "I'd better check he's not a serial absconder, eh?" Lucy was home; he was relieved; but he also felt as if he had been punched in the stomach: Ellie was right, it was all true, his children were at the edge of his life, where he had left them for so many years... "No, he's got no previous convictions, I can bail him." He turned to Aaron and forced a smile. "Aaron, could you dig out Mr Dunn's property bag for me, and then bring the poor chap out of his cell?"

3

Kittens. Hedgehogs in teacups. Rose was looking at Annette McAllister's Facebook page. She had shared a video of a puppy trying to eat snow, a gif of a ginger cat wearing clothes, and a picture of a red panda sitting on someone's shoulder eating a slice of apple, holding it clumsily but endearingly in its paw.

There was nothing personal, nothing about herself or Jack, and Jack himself wasn't on Facebook, or Twitter, or Instagram. Rose gave up and looked again at PC Lohan's statement. *MRS MCALLISTER stated that she was pregnant, but MR MCALLISTER stated that she was not.*

The door of the CID office swung open, and Rose looked up across the empty desks to see Hal and Sophie coming in.

Butland swung around in his chair. "Hey, how did it go with Carl's parents?"

Hal and Sophie came deep into the room, dropping bags and jackets and tablets on to their desks, Hal glancing at his phone. "Not so great," said Sophie, and she slid into her chair and looked up at Hal expectantly. Hal tucked his phone into his pocket and, sighing, rested his hands on the back of his chair, drumming his fingers, and making reluctant eye contact with Rose. He looked a little flushed.

"It went badly," he confessed.

Rose made sympathetic noise.

"They were, it's fair to say, outraged," he elaborated.

"Outraged?" questioned Rose.

"Outraged."

"Outraged at his death?"

"No. Well, yes, they were pretty upset about that, obviously, but they were outraged at my suggestion that he and Georgia were anything other than blissfully happy and in love."

"Oh."

"And I wasn't heavy-handed, I didn't go in there accusing her - well, I was just asking…" He looked down at his hands on the back of the chair. "They didn't want to hear it."

"They were furious," added Sophie. She seemed quite amused. "They practically threw us out."

"So what exactly did you ask them?" questioned Rose, gently.

Hal looked uncomfortable. "I asked whether Georgia and Carl had a history of big rows, whether they threw things or got, well, physically violent with one another… whether Georgia had ever hurt Carl, whether she could have lost her temper and done this."

"They said it was an insult to his memory," put in Sophie.

"I tried to talk about his hospital admissions," Hal went on, "but by that point they were quite agitated."

Butland laughed. "You've put your foot in it there, mate," he said. "Upsetting the victim's parents."

"Mr Lane asked us to leave," Sophie said.

Butland laughed and rocked in his chair.

"So do they think the McAllisters killed him?" asked Rose.

Hal shrugged. "They do - but just because they're certain it wasn't Georgia. They don't know the

McAllisters, don't know anything about them." He looked down at his hands again. "They're in shock. They don't know anything useful."

"Don't feel bad," said Rose. "It was worth a shot. And they might be wrong about Georgia and Carl - it's perfectly possible that Georgia was violent but Carl kept it from his parents."

"They said they were close to him," Sophie said. "He and Georgia visited regularly."

"That doesn't mean they had any idea of what the marriage was like," said Rose. "Don't worry, Hal: when they calm down they'll realise you had to ask those questions. You were doing your job. You were being thorough."

Hal looked at her gratefully.

"I might have something," said DC Ehlen.

There was a pause. Ehlen spoke up so rarely that it seemed to take time for everyone to tune in to the frequency of his voice. Slowly, they all turned to look at him. He was sitting hunched at his desk, as usual, his jacket pulled tightly across his shoulders and his face close to his computer screen. One hand was clutching his can of fizzy orange and the other was gripping his mouse.

"What have you got?" asked Rose.

"I managed to obtain Annette McAllister's work rota," he began. "They have admin people working twenty-four hours, and they were helpful. I cross-referenced her shifts with Carl Lane's hospital admissions. All of the incidents which led to him being admitted to Accident and Emergency occurred at times when she wasn't working."

Rose nodded slowly.

"I haven't been able yet to get hold of Georgia's work records," he went on, "or Jack McAllister's; but from the nature of his work I think we can make the assumption that he works Monday to Friday, nine to five; with the exception of the Boxing Day incident, Carl Lane's injuries all occurred on weekdays when it is likely Jack was working. So these were incidents when Jack was at work and Annette wasn't." He looked up from his screen. "It will be interesting to correlate them with Georgia's work patterns."

"It will," said Rose. "Presumably you can get on to her employer in the morning."

"I also analysed the Facebook and Instagram posts of Carl Lane and Annette McAllister," Ehlen continued. "I discovered that Annette always, without exception, likes Carl's posts, whereas he never likes hers."

Rose raised her eyebrows. "So you think…?"

DC Ehlen looked up again. "Maybe she was attracted to him, but he rejected her. Or maybe they were having an affair and he was more discreet; maybe he challenged her about her indiscretion. Or perhaps they were having an affair and she wanted them to leave their respective spouses, but he wanted the affair to end."

"Maybe," said Rose, slowly. She thought for a moment. "That's good work. We've got a lot to put to Annette. Hal, have you seen PC Lohan's new statement?"

"No."

"Here, have a read." She moved away from her computer so Hal and Sophie could crowd in and look at her screen. "Annette seems to change her mind every few minutes."

Rose stood up, and took a step back while they were reading. She looked at her team. The long low office felt airless and bleak; there was no comfort or encouragement here. She had to pull her team together. She had to give them confidence and courage - this case was becoming a demoralising failure, and although she might not be able to prevent the failure, she could save them from being crushed by it. They needed to feel that they had worked hard and well. "Right then," she said, "we need to focus on Annette. For what it's worth, I still see Georgia as the prime suspect, but we need to shelve that for now and think about Annette McAllister. She's odd, and she's inconsistent - what is she hiding? Let's say she stabbed him. How do we catch her out?"

Hal stood up straighter. "We tell her Carl had a thing for her. We encourage her to see herself as a romantic hero; she seemed to like that idea before. We let her see herself as a passionate woman."

"That's good."

"We question her more," said Sophie, "and get more lies out of her."

"Absolutely."

"We ask her about her visits to Carl when Georgia and Jack were at work," said Butland. "And we ask her directly why she lost her temper, why she attacked him."

"That's good. We accept the reality of an affair and a lovers' tiff."

"We hint that we know she's attacked him on previous occasions," Hal said. "We make it sound reasonable for her to lose her temper sometimes. We sympathise."

"That's right," said Rose. "We'll put to her the new evidence Tomas has come up with. We'll be understanding: we'll say it must have been difficult having these feelings for Carl, being in love, not knowing where she stood…"

"A crime of passion," Butland put in, grinning.

"That's it," Rose said. "Let's get a confession on this before dawn, shall we?" She touched Hal's shoulder. "Let's go and question her again."

They set off along the corridor and down into the stairwell. Rose was shocked to see the patch of sky outside the window. It was, subtly, a shade lighter than it had been before. The sun was still below the horizon, but it was approaching, ineluctably, like a train in the distance making the rails in the station sing and the passengers on the platform creep forward to meet it. Morning was coming. Soon, the thin crackling blinds in the CID office would be yanked upwards and the daylight would be revealed; DCI Newlyn would arrive, freshly ironed and fierce with energy and purpose. The morning would strike Rose like a spotlight, and she would have to perform. She gripped the handrail as she descended the stairs.

On the final flight, within sight of the deep door at the bottom, Hal said: "I'll tell the DCI it was me that upset Mr and Mrs Lane. I handled the situation badly."

Rose paused with her hand on the door. "Don't worry," she said. "The DCI will have the bigger picture on his mind." She looked at Hal. "You didn't do anything wrong. You were pursuing an important line of enquiry."

"Yeah." Hal pulled a face. "But I was clumsy. You'd have done a better job. You're more circumspect, more thoughtful. You wouldn't have gone in like a charging bull."

Rose smiled. "I'm sure you weren't anything like a charging bull."

"I was a bit. I was too single minded. I assumed they would hate Georgia - I was so convinced there was a history of violence."

"You might yet be proved right."

Hal managed a smile. "Maybe. But for now, we're charging at Annette, aren't we?"

4

Nick had just put the phone down from explaining to PC James that Brian Dunn had been bailed when it rang again.

"Custody."

"Nick, is that you?"

"Ellie?"

"I just wanted to say I'm sorry."

The custody suite was, for once, quiet. Aaron was bumbling around in the corridor and all the inmates were silent. Nick took the phone into the kitchen and looked at the taps. "That's okay," he said. "We were both stressed out."

"It was horrible," Ellie said. "When she came back, we had a row. I should have just hugged her and told her I loved her, but instead I started shouting at her."

"You'd been out of your mind with worry," Nick said. "It's natural that you shouted at her. And she knows you love her. You're a great mum."

"She's a good kid… but I was so worried. Anything seems possible in the middle of the night, doesn't it?"

"You'll be able to talk to her properly in the morning."

"Yes. I will. Anyway, I just wanted to say sorry for having a go at you."

"No, you were right. I've never been much of a father. I've always been absent."

"Oh, I wouldn't say that. You've always been around; the kids know you care about them. I think it's more that you're, well… guarded. Not really distant… it's more that you put a barrier up. Not just with me and the kids; you don't get close to anyone, really."

"Well… I don't know."

"All these years since we split up you've stayed single."

"Well, I guess I haven't really met anyone."

"You haven't allowed anyone to meet you. You hide yourself away. You don't take any risks… that's not a criticism, I just mean, you know, don't miss out on life."

"I won't."

"Sorry, I'm tired, I'm just saying stuff…"

There was a noise behind Nick, and he turned to see Rose and her colleague coming up to the desk. "Just a moment," he said into the mouthpiece, and then covered it with his hand and stepped out of the kitchen. "And what can I do for you?"

Rose smiled at him. "We want to interview Annette again."

"Go on then, I might allow that." He flashed a grin and then ducked away to speak into the phone. "I've got to go. Thanks for ringing."

"That's okay."

"Try to get some sleep."

"I will."

He rang off, and called to Aaron to fetch Annette McAllister. "Are you okay?" Rose asked.

"Yes," he said. "She came home."

"That's brilliant."

"It's a relief."

"And it seems to have calmed down here."

"It has. It's positively boring."

"Sounds good."

Aaron brought Annette in, rustling in her paper suit.

"Any particular interview room?"

"Take your pick. They're all free."

Rose grinned at him, and she and her colleague led Annette away. Aaron jangled his keys and muttered something about doing some checks. Nick nodded, and turned to the computer to make a note of Annette's interview on her custody record. He was enjoying the peace, but he was thinking, too, that Ellie was right. He was cautious. He lived his life without risk. His marriage had ended with minimal pain and he had felt lucky; he had slipped out of it relatively unscathed and part of him was afraid that it would be tempting fate to risk a relationship again. He had made his home a safe, solitary nest, and all he was doing there was growing older. Perhaps it was time to emerge, and to take his chances in the world.

He was just turning to check the whiteboard when he heard running steps in the corridor.

He looked up in surprise, as Aaron appeared in the doorway. His normally placid face was white, wide-eyed and open-mouthed. Even before he spoke, Nick's throat clenched. Something terrible had happened.

5

In the interview room, windowless and deep in the basement of the police station, Rose was once again under brutal electric light, hidden from the impending dawn and sealed off from the world. The room was airless, and the smell was an alloy of human sweat and cleaning chemicals. Annette sat on the bench opposite them, her small hands interlaced in front of her, as inscrutable as before. Her slow blink made Rose think of a lizard. The white paper suit, much too big for her and bunched up around her, had the look of a chrysalis, within which she might be taking on any form. Her face, small and mild, looked up at them expectantly; she bit her chapped lower lip, nervously, but only as nervous as a child about to perform in class. She gave her details for the camera again, placidly.

"We have to speak to you again, Annette," Rose began, "because we have new information."

She allowed a pause, but Annette's expression didn't change. Rose looked down at her notes. At the top she had scribbled *Theory: Annette and Carl were having an affair. He rejected her - wouldn't leave his wife? ended affair? - she lost her temper. Alternative theory: Annette was pursuing Carl - maybe she imagined something that wasn't there - he rejected her - ridiculed her? - she lost her temper. Evidence? Her lies.*

"Do you remember, Annette, the police officer who arrested you? His name is PC Lohan."

Annette frowned as if she was trying to picture a face.

"He told us what you said when he got to Carl's house, before Carl was taken away in the ambulance," Rose went on. She scrolled through PC Lohan's statement. Her tablet computer was as slow and intransigent as Annette. "He says... he says: *I turned to Mrs McAllister and asked her what had happened. She said: 'I don't know. He fell on the knife.'* Do you remember saying that?"

Annette pursed her lips and slowly shook her head. "I really don't know. I was so upset, I don't know what I said. Poor Carl was bleeding - it was horrible. I was in a state... But I'm sure that police officer wouldn't lie."

Rose nodded. "So first of all you said Carl fell on the knife. Then the paramedics arrived, and PC Lohan took you and Jack and Georgia into the sitting room of the house. So, you were all there in the sitting room, and PC Lohan says: *At this point Mrs McAllister told me that Ms Lane had stabbed Mr Lane. I asked her if she had seen it happen and she said yes. Ms Lane then turned on Mrs McAllister, calling her an evil liar.* Do you remember that?"

Annette bit her lower lip and turned her head steadily from side to side. "Gosh, I don't know... I mean, we were all pretty upset, Georgie might have said that..."

"Did you tell PC Lohan that you saw Georgia stab Carl? Because PC Lohan is sure that's what you said."

"I don't know. Maybe."

"*Did* you see Georgia stab Carl?"

"Well, no."

"But you told PC Lohan that you did."

"I really can't remember."

"So... after saying he fell on the knife, you then said you saw Georgia stab him. Then PC Lohan arrested all three of you, and he brought you and Jack here to the police station in his car - do you remember that?"

"Yes. Yes, I do. In a police car."

"That's right. PC Lohan says: *While we were in the vehicle Mrs McAllister stated that she was pregnant, but Mr McAllister stated that she was not.*" Rose looked up at Annette. "Do you remember that?"

"Um, I don't know."

"Are you pregnant?"

"Um, I don't know." Her mouth twitched into a coy smile, and she looked down at her hands. "We're trying for a baby, you see…"

"Do you have any reason to believe you are actually pregnant?"

"Well, no…"

"So you weren't telling PC Lohan the truth."

"Well. I suppose I meant I *might* be pregnant."

"I see. PC Lohan goes on: *Mrs McAllister then started to cry and stated that Ms Lane had stabbed Mr Lane but that she hadn't meant to.*"

"Well, I'm sure she didn't mean to. I still believe she loved him. It's all very sad."

"So in the space of less than an hour you went from saying that he fell on the knife, to saying that you saw Georgia stab him, to saying Georgia stabbed him but didn't mean it. You said a lot of different things, Annette."

"Well, I was upset and confused. It was all confusing, and horrible. I don't know what I said."

Rose nodded. "So you were brought here at about five o'clock, and you were put in a cell - and you had time to calm down and think about what had happened. Did they give you a cup of tea? In your cell?"

"Oh, yes," agreed Annette.

"And food - they gave you a meal, didn't they? To eat in your cell? Just a microwave meal, nothing fancy."

"Oh yes," said Annette, eagerly. "It was chilli con carne. It wasn't spicy."

"That's right," said Rose. "So you had time to calm down and sober up, get your head in order. And then, at 23:55, that's nearly midnight - a lot of time had passed - we came to ask you questions, do you remember? In this very room, it was."

Annette nodded. "Yes."

"And we asked you what had happened, and you said that Georgia had got cross with Carl and stormed off into the house, and Carl followed her in, and then there was a noise, and you went into the kitchen and Carl had been stabbed, so Georgia must have done it."

"Yes."

"So at that point you were saying Georgia did it but you didn't see her do it."

"Yes."

"And you said you wouldn't want to have to say that in court."

"Well, I wouldn't."

"Why?"

"Well…"

"Because it's not true."

"No… no, it is true, I just don't want to give evidence against Georgia."

"Why?"

"Well, she's… she's a friend."

"But if she killed Carl?"

"Well, I don't know. I didn't *see* her do it."

"But you told PC Lohan you did."

"Oh, I don't know." Annette started to twist her wedding ring around and around. "It's just so upsetting."

"After we interviewed you, you went back to your cell, and a bit later Carl sadly died. And then a police officer came to your cell to arrest you for murder, and you told him that you'd thought of something new. Some important new information."

Annette said nothing, but kept twisting her ring, the fingers of her left hand held out stiffly.

"So we interviewed you again, in this room, and *this* time you said that there was a burglar in the house. You'd not mentioned this at all before, but suddenly you remembered that there was a noise in the kitchen, and that was why Carl went in, and somehow an intruder had managed to stab him and disappear before the rest of you got there."

Annette looked down at her hands. "Well, I don't know," she said. "I was trying to help."

"You see, Annette, what's obvious here is that you keep telling us completely different things, don't you? You're changing your story every five minutes. And that can only mean one thing." She looked steadily at Annette. "It means you've got something to hide.

"Haven't you?"

She left a pause, and looked hard into Annette's eyes.

Annette's eyes widened. "You think I killed him?"

"Why else would you tell all these lies?"

"They're not lies." Annette suddenly looked tearful. "I'm trying to help; I just get confused. It's all been so horrible."

"You see, your fingerprints are on the handle of that knife."

"But, I told you, I tried to help Carl. And I used the knife to cut lemons."

"Georgia told us that Carl was in the kitchen cutting lemons, and she went inside and upstairs, to fix her hair and makeup. She was upstairs a long time. While she was upstairs, you went in to the kitchen. Jack was in the garden. You went into the kitchen because it was your opportunity to have a private conversation with Carl. Because you were in love with him, weren't you?"

Annette looked at her with surprised eyes. "I liked him," she said carefully, "as a friend. I wouldn't say... I wasn't *in love* with him." Her big eyes glistened again. "Poor Carl."

"You were upset, weren't you? What did Carl say to upset you?"

Annette shook her head. "No. It wasn't anything like that. When I went into the kitchen he'd been stabbed, and Georgia was there. It wasn't anything to do with me."

"We have other evidence," Rose said. She looked down at her scribbled notes. "Carl's been hurt before, hasn't he?"

She looked up at Annette. Annette looked blank. Rose had the feeling that she was pushing against a rock; or foolishly trying to open a sturdy door by kicking at it. Or breaking concrete with a teaspoon. She was getting nowhere. "Let's talk about the tenth of February, earlier this year. Carl had to go to hospital because he hurt his wrist, and his face - he had bruising to his face. You were with him that day, weren't you? We have your work records. Jack was at work, Georgia was at work - but you weren't, were you?"

Annette frowned. "I don't know. The tenth of February? I can't remember."

"How did Carl get hurt?"

"I don't know."

"It was snowy. You went to visit him. You had a fight, didn't you?"

Annette was shaking her head. "I've never had a fight with Carl," she said. "I don't know what you're talking about. Did Georgie say this? Does she think we were having an affair? I only popped round a few times when she wasn't there, we just chatted, that's all. And I don't remember Carl going to hospital."

"Last summer - the fifteenth of July. Again, you weren't at work, Georgia was, Jack was. You saw Carl, didn't you? And you argued. He had to go to hospital again, he thought he'd broken his arm. He had bruising to his arm and his hand."

Annette looked incredulous. "You think this had something to do with me? That's silly."

"It's not silly," said Rose, although she suddenly felt very silly. She felt as if she had wandered outside in her underwear. She was pursuing the weakest line of questioning anyone had ever pursued in the history of policing. She felt useless, utterly ineffectual, doggedly stamping forwards. "Look, Annette, we know about you and Carl. It would be best if you told us now what happened. If you were upset, if he did something to upset you... it's better if you tell us now."

Annette looked at her, blinked, and then slowly shook her head. She didn't look tearful any more. "You think I stabbed him. That's just silly. He was a friend... just a neighbour, really. I didn't know him that well. I was in the garden when it happened, and so was Jack."

She looked down at her hands and shook her head. "I don't want to have to say it, but of course it was Georgia who stabbed him. I don't really know anything about their relationship. Maybe she didn't mean it, maybe it was a moment of madness - maybe she regrets it now. But it was Georgia who did it."

6

They ran down the corridor. Aaron had left the cell door ajar. The doors were thick and heavy, and had always reminded Nick of doors in submarines, not so much closed as sealed. Aaron pushed through and Nick followed.

At first, it struck him that the cell was empty. Expecting to see horror, his stomach lurched at the absence of it. But of course, she was behind the door.

He followed Aaron into the small cell, and they rounded the door, to where a figure hung like a coat on the back of it. Having rushed to her, they both instinctively hesitated now that they had reached her. Aaron then stood back and rubbed his nose, making it clear that this was Nick's business; his job was done now that he had summoned his master. Nick stepped up to her.

"Alice!" he heard himself calling, urgently. "Alice!"

She had used her t-shirt. The top half of her body was naked except for a white bra, and the t-shirt was twisted around her neck and somehow tied to the grille of the door. Nick fumbled to release her, tugging at the taut fabric and plucking at the metal grille; somehow, she fell into his arms, and he lowered her down. "Alice," he said again, wretchedly.

She was cold, and pale. Pallor mortis. There was as yet no rigor mortis: her limbs fell loosely as he lifted her, like the limbs of a sleeping child. She was as light as a child, too, small and bony, and her skin was soft; but she was cold, as cold as a doll.

He lowered her to the floor, and the back of her head banged against the concrete. He didn't want to look at her face. The fabric was still tight around her throat, entangled like an unfathomable scarf, and he tried to tear it. It was frustrating that something as easy to rip as a cheap and flimsy t-shirt could become as resistant as a rope. "Scissors!" he snapped at Aaron. "Fetch scissors! And call an ambulance!"

Yanking down the fabric, he tried to find a pulse at her throat. With two fingers he jabbed at her white flesh, searching for the carotid artery. It was hard to separate out the thumping of his own blood in his ears, but he could feel nothing beneath his fingertips, and knew there was nothing. She was cold and translucent white.

He had to look into her face. Her eyes were not quite closed. Below each bloodless lid there was a glimpse of opaque white eyeball. In dying, even her eyes no longer cared about privacy. Her lips too were parted, and her chin hung low; her whole face was slack and careless. Her body offered no resistance as he handled her. She had the flat, skinny body of a young girl; her bra was a shiny, cheap white nylon against the matt white of her skin, and her hip bones showed as little points in her blue jeans.

He held his hand above her nose and mouth to feel for the touch of breath. Nothing. He moved his hand lower, and then he had to move in his face, to try his sensitive cheek close to her lips. He felt only cold.

He heard Aaron's return, the skid of his shoes on the floor of the corridor, and he took the large clumsy scissors. "Ambulance coming," Aaron muttered. "I'll go let them in." He skidded back into the corridor. Nick gently cut away the t-shirt, carefully sliding the thick blunt back of the blade against Alice's soft neck. It was satisfying to release the clumsy ligature, but he knew it was too late. The exposed hollow of her throat was blue.

He carefully straightened her shoulders, tilted her chin and began compressions on her chest, his hands clasping one another and his arms straight. *One - two - three - four* he counted. The building around him was silent. *Nine - ten - eleven - twelve*. The cell smelled of bleached floor and raw humanity. *Seventeen - eighteen - nineteen - twenty*. He reached thirty and bent over her face. He pinched her nose with one hand, feeling the bone and cartilage beneath the cold skin, and gently put his lips against hers, to breathe into her. Once, twice. He rose up again and repeated the compressions. *One - two - three - four*. It was like a rowing a boat, or swimming - a steady, heaving rhythm, but fast, as intense and energetic as life itself. *Thirteen - fourteen - fifteen - sixteen*. Counting as he moved, the teen numbers seemed to slow him down, their multiple syllables dragging on him. He got to thirty and forced his breath into her again.

He had never known the building to be so quiet. He was alone with her. Kneeling on the floor, he was close to the metal toilet bowl that was attached to the wall and the low vinyl mattress on the wooden bench. There was a cold pain pressing into his knees from the hard floor. *Five - six - seven - eight*. He thought of his daughter, skipping with a rope, counting out loud. *Nine - ten - eleven - twelve*. His own breaths, fast, seemed to be trying to keep time with his counting. *Twenty-five - twenty-six - twenty-seven - twenty-eight*. Almost out of breath, he had to marshal his own lungs to breathe into her again. Her hair was pulled back tightly from her face and he was so close to her hairline that he could see each individual follicle, each delicate dark strand sprouting from the smooth white scalp. He raised himself up and bringing his hands together again, like a double fist, he began again to count.

One - two - three - four. There was no response from her. She was gone, and he was crouched on the floor beside the useless thing she had left behind.

Thirteen - fourteen - fifteen - sixteen.

Twenty-nine - thirty. He leaned in to her face again. He felt that he could do this forever, that he would do this forever. Who was it - Atlas? - whose burden was to forever carry the world on his shoulders? Nick would never stop this: thirty presses, two breaths, thirty presses, two breaths, over and over, so that the event horizon of Alice's death could never be crossed.

One - two - three - four.

Again.

And again.

And again.

Then there was noise echoing down the corridor, as if coming to him from far down a long tunnel; and then the paramedics burst into the room. Nick yielded to them. It was hard to stand up: his legs were stiff and there was pain in his lower back and shoulders as he straightened. It was as if he had been for hours in an attitude of intense prayer. His knees still felt as if something cold and hard was pressing against them. He had to touch the wall to steady himself.

There were two paramedics, both women, in starched green uniforms, efficiently laying out their kit, unzipping boxy bags. They spoke to Alice in loud commands and to each other in familiar mumbles. It had become crowded in the cell and Nick moved back, his lower legs colliding with the bench. For the first time he felt dizzy and nauseous. The paramedics' equipment smelled of disinfectant and plastic. There were other people in the corridor now, and even a voice shouting from another cell. Nick stood with his calves pressed against the edge of the bench and his outstretched fingers touching the wall, giving the women as much space as he could.

The older woman turned her face up to look at him, and shook her head.

"I don't think we can do anything," she said quietly.

Nick nodded.

They manoeuvred a stretcher into the cell and awkwardly loaded Alice onto it. The room was so full of clumsy movement and bulky equipment that Nick had to slide across to the wall and press himself against it. He was trapped there, the space between him and the door filled with activity. The older paramedic was giving instructions - "Move that" - "Lift there" - "Steady" - and it seemed to take them an age to arrange Alice on the complicated stretcher and then manhandle it from the room, like an oversized sofa through a narrow doorway. "Stop" - "Back a bit" - "Could you move out of the way, please?" It seemed that people had accumulated in the corridor.

And then they were gone, clattering away, and Nick was released from the wall. He was left alone in the cell, with just the crumpled, cut t-shirt, and a pair of scissors, on the floor.

7

Rose came out of the interview room and into a swirl of activity and excitement.

"What's going on?"

"Suicide," someone said.

The back door was open, so Rose and Hal took Annette through to the main custody area. There was a uniformed officer at the desk making a phone call but no sign of Nick. Down in the cells, someone was shouting, and some paramedics were rattling a stretcher out of the building. Rose felt for Nick. A suicide was just about the worst thing that could happen to a custody sergeant.

"Who is it?" asked Annette. "Has someone killed themselves? Who is it?"

"Just stay calm," said Rose. For a moment, she looked stupidly at the list of names on the whiteboard, as if the suicide would be recorded there like a delayed plane on an automated screen. Out in the corridor she could hear the voice of the station's duty inspector giving slow and deliberate instructions.

"But who is it? I need to know."

The custodian, Aaron, came in to the room and headed to the desk.

"Aaron!" called Rose. "Who is it?" She nodded her head towards the cells. "Is it one of ours?"

"Alice Delaney," said Aaron, stoutly. "Hanged herself."

"Who was that?" said Annette, querulously.

"Alice Delaney," Rose repeated. "No-one you know."

"Oh, thank goodness."

"Aaron," said Rose. "Could you put Annette back in her cell? Then we can get out from under your feet." There was no sign of Nick.

Aaron looked impassive for a moment and then nodded and took Annette by the arm.

"Let's get out of here," said Hal.

There were uniformed officers coming down the stairwell as Rose and Hal made their way up. Earlier, the building had seemed almost deserted, but the commotion in the cells had reverberated through the floors above and now everyone was emerging from sleepy offices to see what was happening. Footsteps scuffled and voices echoed on the stairs. Through the uncovered window Rose could see that daylight had finally stretched itself out; the early, surprising daylight of summer catching the world still asleep. After yesterday's heat the sky had clouded over, and a motionless, empty white hung over a shadowless, empty town.

Butland was occupying the doorway of the CID office, holding the door open against the will of its wide-elbowed spring. "Is it true?" he asked. "A suicide in custody? Is it one of ours?"

"No," said Rose, as she and Hal slipped past him.

"It's a woman though, isn't it? A hanging."

"Yes, it's a woman, and a hanging."

"Jesus. Someone'll be in the shit for that."

Rose sat down wearily.

"What did Annette say?" asked Sophie.

Rose shook her head. "She doesn't seem to think there's anything wrong with changing her story every five minutes."

"Maybe she's mentally ill," said Sophie.

"Personality disorder," said Butland. "Compulsive liar."

"No court will believe her," said Hal.

"Which is bad news for us," said Rose. "Really bad news."

The others looked at her.

"The problem is," she explained carefully, "if we charge Georgia with murder, Annette is our prime witness. She's the one who said Georgia and Carl were arguing. She's the one who said Georgia followed him into the kitchen. But if we call her to give evidence, we'll have to let the defence have all this other material - her interviews, PC Lohan's statement - all her different versions of events. In exploring her lies, we've made her useless to us as a witness."

Hal sighed. "So we're back to square one."

"I don't think we ever really left square one," said Rose.

A glum silence settled on the room, and she felt guilty; she tried to think of something positive to say, but every thought she pursued took her to a dead end. Hal, Sophie and Ehlen turned to their computers; Butland started to scroll his phone and rock his chair. Rose sat beneath the harsh lights and looked at her useless notes. She could sense surrender approaching with the morning.

She thought about Nick and the awful time he was having right now, many floors below. Poor Nick, with his comfortable girth and his biscuits and his whiteboard;

no-one was safe. She wished she could reach out to him and offer words of comfort. Her mother had at one time believed in psychic powers, and had told her children that when they were at school she was projecting a ring of love and protection around them from afar; Rose had never really believed her mother had paranormal abilities but it was nice to know she was loved. She could imagine the invisible shell of light around herself, rainbow-smeared and translucent like a giant soap bubble. Now, she thought about Nick, far below, and she tried to mentally extend her warmth for him like a consoling touch.

"Hey, this is interesting," said Sophie. She was reading an email.

"What?" asked Rose.

"It's the report on that Rolling Stones record cover," Sophie went on. "They found Carl's fingerprints on it, but mainly they found Jack McAllister's. His prints are all over it, like he was the last person to handle it."

Rose tapped her desk.

"That puts him in the kitchen," she said, thoughtfully. "He said he only passed through the kitchen to get to the garden, but this puts him in there properly."

"Another straw to clutch at," said Hal.

"Well," said Rose, "we need to interview him anyway, to see what he has to say about Annette's lies. Hal, could you call up his solicitor and get him in? That's assuming we can get near an interview room with the circus going on downstairs."

8

Rose looked at the clock.

"The time is seven minutes past six," she said. She saw Sam Stead jot down the time in his notebook; he had already started to draw angular doodles around the date. "We just need to ask you some more questions, Jack. We have some more evidence, and it seems we're beginning to get to the bottom of what happened." She wished she wasn't bluffing.

Jack McAllister looked across the table at her and rubbed his nose. His eyes were pink and his lips were pinched and tense. "I have this to show you," Rose said, and she pulled out the Rolling Stones record.

It was encased in a clear plastic bag, and she laid it flat in the table and smoothed out the wrinkled plastic so everyone could see the cover. "Have you seen this before, Jack?"

Jack scratched his beard. "I guess so, yeah, yeah, Carl showed it to me."

"That's right," said Rose. "It has your fingerprints all over it." She paused. "It was in the kitchen, Jack."

Jack nodded.

"You told us, Jack, that you only walked through the kitchen to get to the garden. You said you only came back into the kitchen *after* Carl had been stabbed. So when did he show you this record?"

"I don't… I, well, I guess he showed it to me, I guess it must've been in the kitchen."

"So you were in the kitchen with Carl, before he was stabbed."

"I don't... well, yeah."

"Just the two of you."

Jack was looking at the record. "Yeah," he said.

"Where was Annette when he showed you this record?"

"She was in the garden."

"And where was Georgia?"

Jack shrugged. "She was upstairs," he said, sullenly.

Rose could feel Hal shift beside her on the bench. They had a scent here, a glimpse of their quarry. Rose needed to step carefully. "Why did he show you this record?"

"I guess he was just, you know, showing it to me, out of interest..." Jack shook his head, and then added, with sudden vehemence: "He was showing off, that's what he was doing. He'd got it for a bargain, he said it was worth thousands and the person he bought it off didn't know. He was, you know, pleased with himself, showing off. That's what Carl was like."

There was a silence. Jack was shaking his head, his eyes still fixed on the record. "You should know," he said. "That's what Carl was like. He wasn't some sort of saint."

"Okay," said Rose. "Jack, we need to talk about Annette."

Jack looked up. "Annette?"

Rose nodded. "Annette's got herself in a right mess."

"What do you mean?"

"She keeps telling lies. Changing her story every five minutes." Rose looked at her notes. "First, she told the police that Carl fell on the knife. Then she said she saw

Georgia stab him. Then she said she was pregnant… all this was before she even got to the police station. And then she came up with this ridiculous story that there was a burglar in the house." Rose looked up at Jack. "She's got herself into a lot of trouble, telling all these lies."

Jack was shaking his head. "She's so bloody stupid," he said.

"It's obvious that Annette is trying to cover something up," Rose went on. "The thing is, Jack, the more you and Annette go on lying, the worse it gets, for both of you."

"You're right." Jack shook his head. "You're right. I don't want Annette to cover for me. You're right, the truth has to come out. I did it. I'm sorry."

"Jack, I think we need a private word," Sam Stead said.

"No, it's okay," Jack said, turning to him. "I'm sorry I lied to you too. I can't keep pretending like this; the truth has to come out sooner or later."

He looked up at Rose. His eyes were wet and pink. "I did it, I stabbed him - I can't believe it, even now - but I didn't mean it, I mean, I didn't plan to… I was drunk, it was just… I tried to save him. I knew not to pull out the knife. I pressed a tea towel against the wound. I tried to stop the bleeding. I'm so sorry, I never meant to kill him - it was a moment of madness, you know?"

"Tell us exactly what happened," said Rose, gently. "You were all in the garden, and Carl went inside, yes? Into the kitchen."

"Yeah." Jack sniffed. "He went in, and then Georgia said she was going to freshen up. That's the kind of thing she says, 'freshen up'. Like she's a film star or something." He sniffed again, and rubbed his nose testily. "So she went in, and she must have gone upstairs to powder her nose or whatever, and then Carl comes to the door and he calls me in, said he wanted to show me something..." He looked at Rose as if he was trying to make her understand. "That's what he was like. He called me into the kitchen like I was a puppy or something, like I was a *fan* of his... he was always like that, behaving like me and Annette were lucky to know him. Like we were lucky that him and Georgia were bothering to talk to us, you know? Like they were the beautiful people and we were the plebs."

He was looking at Rose so intently that she had to nod sympathetically.

"So I went in, and he started showing me this Rolling Stones record he'd got. He was going on about how it was worth thousands, he was really smug about it. And he gave it to me to look at, to hold, like he was doing me a favour, you know? Like he was letting me touch his treasures." Jack rubbed his nose angrily again. "And then he took it off me, and he put it on the side, and then he said, he said something about showing it to 'little wifey' - that's what he used to call Annette. Not to her face, it's what he called her when it was just him and me - 'little wifey' - he used to say things like 'haven't you got little wifey pregnant yet?' - things like that."

He sniffed. "Annette had, you know, a bit of a thing for him, it was so obvious, she's such a silly cow... he thought it was hilarious, you know? It was embarrassing. So I - oh, I was, I was drunk, I'd just had enough of him, he thought he was so great - I just, I just picked up the knife that was right there, next to me, and I think I just wanted to scare him really, to show him he wasn't so, so… I don't know… but I was angry and a bit drunk and I kind of lashed out."

He looked Rose in the eyes. "I didn't mean to kill him, I swear, it was just a stupid, spur of the moment thing. It happened so quickly…" He shook his head. "I don't know. I just lashed out with a knife in my hand."

"Was it a slash or a stab?" asked Hal.

"I don't know… like this."

He held up his arm and mimed a wild, reckless, angry motion. It would have carried sufficient force to plunge the knife into Carl's neck.

"And… the knife sort of stuck in him, I mean, I don't know, it happened so quickly… There was all this blood. And he sort of looked at me, in surprise." Jack took a breath. "I really didn't mean to kill him. I was shocked. The knife went really far into his neck and actually stuck there, and then he sort of, sort of keeled over, or more like, crumpled… and I tried to help him. I mean, you can see I didn't want him to die: I tried to help him." He shook his head. "I grabbed a tea towel and I pressed it to the wound, to try to stop the bleeding. I never wanted him to die." He sniffed and looked at his hands.

"What happened then?"

"I guess… I guess Annette must have heard something, because she came in… and then Georgia came downstairs. And she started screaming."

He stopped talking, and rubbed his face with both hands.

"I'm really sorry," he said. "I didn't mean to kill him. It was just, just one of those things, you know?"

9

Daylight.

Nick stood outside the back door, smoking a cigarette. He had allowed the back door to shut. The car park looked startlingly different in daylight: the tall lights were extinguished and the shadows were gone, and instead a diffuse morning light fell gently and evenly, without judgement, on everything - the cars, the tarmac, the weeds, and the coarse pebbledash wall of the building. The air was fresh, neither warm nor cool but as yet playfully undecided; and the sound of birdsong and early traffic was carried on the faintest breath of breeze.

The car park was becoming busy; shifts were changing and people were coming and going, but they used the doors at the side of the building and didn't see Nick in his dip outside the basement. Overhead, the flat white cloud had started to break up into a soft rippled texture, with faint flecks of golden light cast by a shy sun.

Nick was thinking about Alice, who was dead. She had been nineteen, barely an adult, barely begun. She had been an unprotected child, an unloved child, an unformed adult. She was impulsive and volatile and afraid. She was erratic... but in a sense, it was simple cause and effect, wasn't it? He had charged her and remanded her in custody and that had caused her to kill herself. She had said: "I can't do Ripley again." She had wept, and pleaded with him. He had refused her bail.

When had she decided to do it? The lasagne bothered him. He could remember Katrina taking Alice a lasagne, and bringing back the empty plate. What was Alice thinking then? Was she already resolute, asking for a last meal? Was she planning even then how to tie her t-shirt to the grille? Or was she eating because she was a hungry teenager, full of life and future intentions, planning what to say to her solicitor in the morning and working out who she could call to bring her cigarettes and provide her with a bail address, thinking through the schemes and challenges of another day? Was her decision to hang herself a sudden desperate impulse that came much later, an impulse she acted on before it could pass? Did she hope to be found in time - to be saved? Did she want to be rescued? Did she think that the custody sergeant, the steady, reliable man in uniform, the father figure at the end of the corridor, would save her?

He would never know. And he would never know if he could have saved her, if he had checked on her more often, or at a different time.

Everything was coming down on him now: the enquiry, the investigation. The forensic team were already in the cells, moving silently about their work like pallbearers. He would probably be exonerated, but the procedure would be long and slow and painful - there would be serious questioning and ponderous reports - and even if in the end he was absolved of all blame, he would always be a custody sergeant who had allowed a suicide on his watch.

The back door opened, and Nick flinched. Forensic technicians had been coming and going without meeting his eye, although the Station Inspector had been reassuring: "Don't you worry," he kept saying, "you'll be alright." Katrina had come back in the middle of it all, looking more cheerful than she had all shift, not knowing what had happened. "Stuart had a good sleep," she said, tucking back her hair. "He's actually feeling a bit more comfortable. Hey, what's up?"

She had been horrified when Nick told her, not just because Alice was such a familiar face but because she knew she shouldn't have gone home during her shift, leaving him short staffed. Nick could have put all the blame on Katrina, if he was so inclined - he could have denied giving her permission to go. Of course, Nick would never do that. He had already told the Inspector the entire truth. He could have called for a replacement for Katrina, but he didn't, because he knew no-one would be available. "Shame, that," the Inspector had said, gruffly. "It's a shame you didn't call to request a replacement - you'd have covered yourself, at least. Oh well, we can't go back and do things differently, can we?"

"No," said Nick. "We can't go back and do things differently."

He flinched when the back door opened, but it was Rose Olding, unexpectedly, and when she saw him she smiled and gently shut the door behind her. "They said you were still around somewhere," she said.

Nick nodded. "They told me to go home," he said, "but I wanted to stay just in case Forensics had any questions."

Perhaps he was staying as a form of penance; or maybe it was a kind of vigil. Maybe he was hoping for a resolution; although he knew that would take months, not hours. Maybe he just didn't know how to leave.

"How are you doing?" asked Rose.

Nick shrugged. "Not my best shift ever."

"You'll be okay," Rose said. "You know you'll be okay. This happens sometimes - you can't predict every suicide. They were saying in there that this girl had no history of mental illness, nothing flagged, and she was only in for a shed burglary... no-one will blame you."

Nick nodded. "I know."

"Everyone knows how thorough you are. Everyone knows you're one of the best."

Nick returned her smile. "I'll be okay," he said. "Cigarette?"

"Go on then." She took one, and they moved closer together for him to light it.

"Anyway," Nick said, "I heard Jack McAllister confessed."

"He did!" She blew out smoke. "Success. Relief."

"How did you catch him in the end?"

Rose shook her head. "We didn't. We found something that placed him in the kitchen, but it was only vague and circumstantial - he could still have denied being in the kitchen at the material time. We just got lucky - he decided to confess."

"I'm sure it was your clever line of questioning."

Rose laughed. "Not likely. No, he just decided he wanted to hold his hands up to it."

"I suppose he couldn't face a lifetime of carrying a dark secret."

"That's right. Like Lady MacBeth."

"*Exactly* like Lady MacBeth. 'Unnatural deeds do breed unnatural troubles.' She lost her mind pretty quickly." He ground out the stub of his cigarette. "So why did McAllister do it?"

"Oh, the stupidest of non-reasons... Carl was successful, boastful, arrogant; Jack was jealous and drunk... he just saw red. It's mad, isn't it? Mad and sad. Carl Lane was murdered just for being a bit irritating."

Nick nodded. "Happens all the time. Fights over trivial things, pointless deaths."

Rose flicked her ash. "Human beings are so fragile."

" 'Life's but a walking shadow; a poor player, that struts and frets his hour upon the stage, and then is heard no more; it is a tale told by an idiot, full of sound and fury, signifying nothing,' " said Nick. Then he laughed. "Sorry, that was a bit grim."

Rose laughed too. "No, that was appropriate."

They both looked at the sky. Gradually, the cloud was melting, and the blue patches were growing. Nick pulled out his cigarettes and lit another one. "Chain smoking?" smiled Rose.

"I think the occasion calls for it," said Nick. "Shouldn't you be in there, taking all the glory for solving a murder?"

Rose laughed. "Actually I'm hiding. We need to release Georgia and take a witness statement from her. Sophie offered to do it - Georgia hasn't met her. I don't think Georgia Lane likes me much after all this." She flicked her ash on the ground. "I told Sophie she can pretend she's only just come on duty. She can be utterly sympathetic and agree that I'm a bitch."

Nick laughed.

"I just glad Sophie volunteered to do it," Rose continued. "I'm a coward." She paused. "I'm lucky. I've got a good team."

"You've *built* a good team."

"Aw, shucks." Rose grinned. "We shouldn't be talking about my good fortune, anyway."

"Yes, we should," said Nick. "It's cheering me up."

"Okay," Rose said. "I'll tell you the best bit. After the interview with Jack, Hal and I went upstairs to the CID office only to find the DCI sat there, scowling and going through the file. He'd said he was coming in at seven, but he came in early to surprise me. So it was great to walk in with a confession. Case solved."

"Perfect timing," smiled Nick.

"It was very satisfying." Rose ground out her cigarette end. Nick offered her another.

"No thanks." She shook her head. "I do need to get on, really - I'm going to interview Annette McAllister again."

Nick raised his eyebrows.

"She must have known Jack did it. I'm going to put his confession to her. I reckon we should be charging her with assisting an offender or obstruction - maybe even perverting the course of justice."

"You *are* on the warpath."

Rose laughed. "Listen," she said, "I was wondering... do you want to go out for a drink some time?"

"Yeah." Nick nodded. "Yeah, I'd like that."

"I'm off on Wednesday... would Tuesday night be good for you?"

"Absolutely."

"Excellent." She had blushed slightly. She turned to the door and laughed. "How do I get back in then?"

Nick laughed too. "You have to ring the bell like a commoner."

Rose rang, and someone inside buzzed her in. "Back to work, then. See you Tuesday."

The door closed behind her, leaving Nick leaning on the rough wall, smoking. Behind the building, the sun must have finally broken through, because golden light was suddenly glinting off the cars at the far end of the car park, beyond the police station's heavy shadow. Above, the streaks of cloud left the patches of blue looking pale and clean. Nick remembered that earlier, when he was frantic with worry about Lucy, he had imagined a moment in the future, when it would all be over and he would be either devastated or relieved. Life had a way of taking surprising turns. He had not imagined this moment at all.

He remembered the feel of Alice, frail and bony, as he lowered her to the ground.

A tale told by an idiot, he thought.

He remembered Joe's visit, the day before - was it really less than twenty-four hours ago? - when they had sat in his kitchen eating buttery bacon sandwiches. Joe was talking about his Maths exam. He was saying how orderly Maths was, compared to English Literature: it was all certainties, answers that were definitely either right or wrong, predictable patterns and logic. "I know," Nick had said. "If only life was like Maths, eh? Neat and tidy and predictable." They had laughed. "It would be boring, though," Joe had added.

Nick finished his cigarette and flattened the end under his boot. He shouldn't feel sorry for himself. Two people had died during the night, senselessly, but he was alive, in this fine, infant day, with a future - his children, Rose - of possibilities. He remembered what Joe had said about taking hold of his own destiny. Life was unreasonable and unpredictable, so the only way to live it was with hope and optimism. Stepping away from the wall, Nick began the new day.

Also by Sarah Healey

The Day of the Trial

Having Fun

Red Blue Green

Lightning Source UK Ltd.
Milton Keynes UK
UKHW010839021218
333301UK00001B/62/P